"What the hell. Nice a day to die as any..."

But if death had Gadgets's number, the Able Team warrior had no intention of twiddling his thumbs waiting for the end.

As he bailed out of the Apache, Gadgets drew more rifle fire from the roof of the hatchery and was forced to dive forward into the brush. Brittle limbs snapped under his weight, and he felt the sting of smaller branches against his face.

He rose to a partial crouch and peered in the direction of the hatchery. Fifteen feet ahead of him, one of the Yellow River Brigade sentries was staring at him over the sights of his M-14.

Mack Bolan's

ABLE TEAM ®

ABLE TEAM.

Cold Steel

Dick Stivers

A GOLD EAGLE BOOK FROM
W🦅RLDWIDE.

TORONTO • NEW YORK • LONDON • PARIS
AMSTERDAM • STOCKHOLM • HAMBURG
ATHENS • MILAN • TOKYO • SYDNEY

First edition October 1988

ISBN 0-373-61238-9

Special thanks and acknowledgment to
Ron Renauld for his contribution to this work.

Printed in U.S.A.

PROLOGUE

It was no ordinary train that coursed through the Great Sandy Desert of Oregon's remote Harney Basin. Six cars long, fronted by a pair of seething diesel engines, the train bore few markings. Property of the United States Army's Fort Shaw military installation in upper Malheur County, the serpentine hulk of rolling steel carried a cargo that begged for discretion.

Missiles.

Two of the longer cars, each stretching more than eighty feet and resting on ten axles, contained unarmed Smallboy MX missiles, among the first built since Congress had voted to appropriate funds for their creation more than two years ago. Other cars contained launch control facilities and mobile traveling quarters for the twenty-four-man security force accompanying the payload. As part of what would eventually become a network of more than two dozen similar rail weapon systems scattered throughout the country, the train was simulating the maneuvers it would be expected to undertake in the event of a major global confrontation between the superpowers. With an estimated 200,000 miles of track spread across the continental United States, the theory was simple: if a potent part of the country's arsenal was put out on the rails, it would be virtually impossible for the Soviets to track down every missile aimed at its heartland. The Russians could possibly take out silo-based Minutemans and Peacekeepers by punching their ICBMs through United States defenses, but there would still be the elusive Smallboys out on the prowl, each packing a single but potent retaliatory warhead. In a world where the balance of power was measured in terms of mutually assured destruction, the rail MX system was looked upon as an essential wild card in the diplomatic equation.

"What a screwed situation," Colonel James Washgan, head of the security detail, groused as he hand-rolled a cigarette with practiced ease despite the jiggling motion of the train. Silver-haired, with a large, square face highlighted by stern gray eyes, Washgan had lied about his age to join the Army as a sixteen-year-old the day after Pearl Harbor. If ever a man looked born for the uniform, it was he. He'd already passed up the opportunity twice to retire with full benefits, and he swore that his only plans for the time after he had outlived his usefulness as an officer were to crawl into a casket and let them hammer down the lid before putting him six feet under.

As he held the flame of a personalized lighter to the tip of his handiwork, Washgan noticed Lieutenant C. W. Texico eyeing him warily. The two men were in the officers' quarters, a small room walled off from the rest of the rolling barracks used by their charges.

"Sir?" Texico questioned. He was young enough to be Washgan's son and looked upon the colonel as a much valued and admired mentor. They'd worked together for three years.

"You heard me." Washgan blew smoke and slapped the lighter shut before slipping it back into his shirt pocket. They were rounding a bend and through the window of their compartment the men could see the back cars of the train trailing thunderously along with the steady, clattering rhythm of wheels passing over the rail links. "Those goddamn missiles have made us damn near obsolete. Sticks in my craw every time I think of it."

"They'll never replace good manpower," Texico offered with half-mustered conviction.

"True," Washgan muttered. "We're needed to push the buttons."

Texico knew the spiel, having heard it plenty of times in the past, not only from Washgan but from other older officers who could recall a time when conventional warfare was the only game in town and strategy invariably boiled down to the implementation of able-bodied soldiers on the field of battle. If your men had the numbers, the guts and the right kind of backup, you could send them in with a reasonable assurance they could bring you victory, or at least do enough damage to increase the odds of winning the overall war at some point down the line. But now manpower, though still touted as a vital component, had waned in importance next to implements of technology. Military hardware now claimed the bulk of focus and funds in Congress. Stacked up against the latest state-of-the-art missiles, bombs, satellites and other hi-tech weaponry, it was easy for a man in a uniform to feel dwarfed and insignificant, especially if he recalled those older, simpler times.

"I keep an eye on the men, sir," Texico said, trying to head off his superior's skepticism. "They still feel like they can make a difference. I don't see or sense a morale problem at all."

"That's good." Only two puffs into his cigarette, Washgan stubbed it out in an ashtray and rose from his chair. "Nice they don't know any better. But shit, what can you do?"

"Persevere," Texico said. Reading Washgan's mood, the lieutenant knew some diversion was in order. He reached to his right and pulled out a deck of cards from the table beside him. "Play some gin, sir?"

"I'd rather drink some," the colonel wisecracked, moving over to a chair across from Texico. "Yeah, go ahead and deal."

Falling silent, the two men busied themselves with the cards, unaware that before the game could be decided, they would both be dead.

FOUR MILES AWAY, twenty-three-year-old Qi Zhayoi stood in the shadow cast by Freezeout Mountain, at 5,485 feet the highest elevation in all of Malheur County. He was a short, wiry man, wearing a leather flight jacket over his khaki slacks and shirt. Dark-tinted aviator glasses shielded his eyes, hiding the uncertainty they held. He paced in a small circle on the sunbaked hardpan, trying to compose himself as he watched his fellow members of the Yellow River Brigade carefully load a Cessna Model 425 Corsair, resting on the flatland like a lost bird. In a few minutes, Qi would be at the controls of that plane, ready to undertake the most delicate flight of his short life. He also knew it would be his last flight, and secretly he prayed for the strength to fulfill his mission and assure himself of the heightened immortality of those who successfully pursue the destiny fate assigns them.

Over the past seven months, the Brigade had assembled munitions from various sources, primarily the black market and several California and Oregon Army depots with lax security. As was the case with almost every scavenger-oriented stockpiling undertaken by terrorists or other underground warriors, the Brigade's haul during that period had included a trove of ammunition that was incompatible with the weaponry that fell into their hands during the same period. The usual course of action was for the group to barter its unusable plunder in hopes of bolstering the arsenal it felt most comfortable implementing. However, in the case of the Yellow River Brigade, it had been decided that this mismatched firepower could be put to better use in turning the Cessna into something of a crude, poor-man's guided missile. In all, the thirty-five-foot-long plane was weighted down with a case of Armbrust ATW antipersonnel fragmentation rounds, another case of .460 Magnum bullets normally intended for use with the Weatherby Mark V rifle, five crates of 200-grain .38-caliber ammo and two crates of 9 mm parabellum, five 30-round .45 ACP cartridges and four boxes of lethal LAW-80 94 mm hollow-charge warheads. Once his cargo was stacked inside the plane, eight half-filled three-gallon canisters of gasoline were stored at strategic points in the cockpit, fuselage and rear of the craft.

With the Cessna readied, the other men retreated from the plane and gathered near two trucks bearing the insignia of the National Forestry Service. The uniforms they wore were likewise attributed to this conservation agency. Although all nine men were of Chinese extraction, they were, like Qi Zhayoi, wearing mirror-lensed sunglasses to conceal their widely spaced eyes. Four of the men had dyed their skin a dusky shade of tan to further mask their Oriental features and the others were light-skinned enough not to draw undue attention to their race. Anyone giving them a casual glance could have easily mistaken them for a typical multiethnic group in the employ of the United States government.

Hannas-ma Yang walked away from the others and approached Qi Zhayoi. At thirty-two, Hannas-ma had distinguished himself over the past six years as one of the Yellow River Brigade's most reliable and ruthless field officers, doing much to help the organization evolve from being no more than an obnoxious gnat buzzing in the ear of the established ruling party in Communist China to a much loathed and equally feared threat to the existing power structure. Taking their name from the untamed watercourse that had played such a significant role in the history of mainland China, the Brigade advocated whatever measures were necessary to unite Red China and the Soviet Union under a common yoke that would allow them to jointly carry out Communist objectives that neither country had thus far been able to achieve alone. Denounced by the current Party Congress as running dogs on the leash of Moscow's politburo, the Yellow River Brigade's homeland activities had been held in check by the diligent efforts of Chinese intelligence and the military. But overseas the outfit thrived in exile, slowly building strength and courting what influence it could in the pursuit of its aims. In the continental United States, Hannas-ma Yang was the man in charge of all Brigade efforts, and in addition to the ten-man team he was commanding today, there were at least a half dozen other pockets of Brigade-backed terrorism being nurtured in other parts of the country.

But Hannas-ma could deal with those others later. For now, a great moment of truth was at hand, and the matter demanded his full attention. Standing before Qi Zhayoi, he placed a hand on the man's shoulder and lowered his sunglasses while telling the pilot to do the same. Eye to eye, the two men stared at each other, then spoke in their native tongue.

"The time has come, Qi."

"Yes," the pilot replied stiffly.

There was nothing more to be said.

Qi slipped his glasses back on and broke away from Hannas-ma, striding purposefully toward the waiting Cessna. He pulled a helmet onto his head and took a long, deep breath, then climbed up and into the cockpit. His destiny was at hand.

"I'M GOING DOWN with four," Colonel Washgan announced, laying his cards out on the table. He grinned happily as he wedged a fresh cigarette between his lips. "Top that, Tex."

The lieutenant looked at Washgan's hand, then set down his own cards, playing two strays off either end of the colonel's heart straight. "Sorry, sir, but that leaves me with only two."

The smile faded on Washgan's face as he stared blankly at the cards. Smoke curled up from his nostrils and out of the corners of his mouth. "Sumbitch," he grumbled.

"You're still twelve points up on me," Texico told his superior as he charted the score.

"So I am." Washgan squinted as smoke stung his eyes. He gathered the cards together and began shuffling them. Despite the last loss, he was in better spirits than he had been before they'd started playing. Gotta learn to take things more in stride, he told himself. Nobody likes an old codger lost in his memories.

"I wonder what kind of new tricks they're working on for the XT-22," he murmured, forcing himself to at least try to keep up-to-date with the latest development of those weapons he felt were making him obsolete.

"Same old concept," Texico said, "only leaner and meaner, from what I hear."

The men were referring to the other strategic cargo they were carrying besides the Smallboys. The XT-22, when rendered fully operable with detonator and plutonium source material, represented the latest breakthrough in nuclear warheads, emphasizing streamlined and lightweight construction as part of the military's never-ending quest for less cumbersome options than current weapon systems. There were six unarmed XT-22s secreted aboard the train, in the railcar with the launch controls for the Smallboys, and once brought to Malstrom Air Force Base in Montana, the warheads would be prepped for use and then slipped down to Nevada for underground testing and evaluation. Ironically, once perfected, the XT-22s would be the cornerstone for a new generation of nuclear arms that would make even the Smallboys outmoded by the mid-1990s.

"Well, I tell ya, I'm gonna have to take a cue from those missiles and get myself leaner and meaner one of these days," Washgan said, giving himself a good-natured slap on the stomach.

"Oh, I think you're mean enough, sir," Texico said with a smirk.

As he was dealing the next hand, Washgan heard the door swing open behind him and turned to see a youthful private burst into the quarters.

"What is it?" Washgan demanded.

"Just picked up something on radar, sir," the younger man reported. "It's headed this way, just high enough to read."

Washgan frowned and set down the cards. He and Texico both knew that airspace over this section of the desert was off-limits to all but restricted personnel. Because the train was carrying only unarmed missiles and warheads, plans for an air escort had been scrapped earlier in the week so that additional jets could be diverted to the latest trouble spot in the Persian Gulf. Whatever was flying toward the train had no clearance to be doing so. The implications were obvious and ominous. Both officers bolted to their feet and followed the private from the small cubicle.

"Code three," Washgan barked as he led the way through the barracks, which was already alive with the activity of soldiers readying for battle stations.

"It's already been called," the private said.

Even as he was speaking, the train jerked sharply as the engines up front had their high-powered brake systems activated. The men braced themselves, holding on to whatever they could to keep from being wrenched off their feet by the train's abrupt stopping power.

"Halloween was last week," Washgan deadpanned as he unsnapped his holster and pulled out a seven-round automatic. "Whoever this trick-or-treater is, they're in for more of a surprise than they were hoping for. Let's get 'em!"

Before he or Texico could leave the railcar, however, there was a second jolt caused by the recoil of an antiaircraft gun mounted on the adjacent car. It missed its target and moments later the entire barracks car was turned into a fiery inferno of hot, twisted metal and bursting ammunition. The low-flying Cessna struck its intended target head-on, obliterating itself as it brought a sudden, scorching death to eighteen of the twenty-four men assigned to guard the train. Washgan and Texico were cremated in a matter of seconds as the derailed car threw off the dark, billowing cloud of a funeral pyre.

THE TWO FORESTRY SERVICE trucks were on the scene less than fifteen minutes later.

"Well done, Qi." Hannas-ma Yang grinned as he stared through the windshield of the lead truck at the still-raging blaze devouring the disabled train's mid-section. "You served the cause well."

Most of the survivors of the calamity were gathered together on the desert hardpan beyond reach of the burning car. Half of them were wounded and either sitting or lying on the ground. They looked stunned from their ordeal, and when Hannas-ma Yang and three of his cohorts climbed out of the

liminary report of their findings, then
aining personnel into two groups, one
ending to the casualties and the other
the train for any clues that might shed
bacle.

e barracks car had been wrenched onto
e two cars attached to either end of it
harp angles, the rest of the train was
adily boardable. Weapons drawn, the
proached doorways and entered the
engines. They quickly ascertained that
though visibly shaken about, were still
y in their portable launch chutes. Sim-
ch controls showed no signs of having
with. But it didn't take long for two
cross the emptied safes and return to
ews that the XT-22 warheads had been

Vebster swore, already imagining the
quences of the theft. He personally put
xt call to Fort Shaw, asking to speak
ommander, General Bill Hedge. When
Hedge let loose with a few choice epi-
n before calming down.

ey weren't loaded," the general's grav-
kled over Webster's radio. "Without
detonators, they're not much good for
oorstops."

w, sir," Webster countered. "Seems to
draw a good price on the black mar-
ntries would like to have that kind of
heir disposal. They could take a few of

trucks, only one of the soldiers had the presence of mind to question the new arrivals.

"We're with the Forest Service," Hannas-ma told the soldier, speaking in a calm, reassuring voice. "We heard the explosion and called it in. What happened?"

The soldier looked to be in his late teens, and his acne-ravaged face was pale with a fear that made his voice quaver as he spoke. "Some plane...some fucking kamikaze. Just plowed right into the barracks car. Musta been twenty guys trapped in there...."

"All dead?" Hannas-ma Yang asked.

"Look!" the soldier whined, pointing at the charred car. "Yes, they're all dead!"

"Have you called for help?"

The soldier shook his head. Tears began to streak down the grime on his cheeks. "All the radios were in there...except for the ones in the engine room. We tried putting out a call, but no luck."

Hannas-ma shook his head in a gesture of sympathy. "Most unfortunate."

The terrorist's next gesture was a hand signal, and the moment it was given, the other members of the Yellow River Brigade poured out of the two trucks, brandishing M-14 rifles, courtesy of an arms transaction with American drug dealers anxious for access to a conduit that could supply them with a steady flow of Chinese opium. Though almost thirty years old, the M-14s were still commendable rifles, prized for their quality operation and accuracy. Within seconds, the Brigade had fanned out and dropped to firing position, ripping a lethal shower of NATO rounds into the unsuspecting survivors at a rate of 750 rounds per minute. Hannas-ma and the other three men dived sharply to one side to be clear of the fire, and one of them became the only victim of American fire, taking a slug to the shoulder from the young soldier who was already dead by the time his finger had squeezed the trigger.

The massacre took less than a minute, and when it was over several of the terrorists came forward to inspect the fatalities while Hannas-ma Yang led the others to the derailed car containing the launch systems for the Smallboys and the XT-22 warheads. As he had hoped, in all the commotion the doors to the railcar had been left unlocked, and they had no trouble getting inside. Opening the security locks protecting the XT-22s was more of a problem, but the Brigade's inside contacts, who had given them the information necessary to stage their raid, had also provided the necessary codes for bypassing the computer lock system. When Hannas-ma opened the thick-plated doors and stared at the packed warheads, a smile crept across his thin lips.

"Yes," he whispered triumphantly. "Yes..."

WITHIN MOMENTS after communications between the train and base quarters at the Shaw military installation had been severed by the jarring impact of the suicide Cessna, base dispatchers had assumed the worst and put out a red alert. At once a number of on-call pilots were scrambling across the runway of the camp's airfield and climbing into Iroquois surveillance helicopters. By the time they had pulled up from the ground and lofted off toward the last known coordi-

nates of the train, an
jet was being pressec
the event it might b
word about the te
spreading to other
American Northwes
taken to ensure tha
unnecessarily vulne
that the situation es

Isolated as the H
were the first to rea
six minutes after t
smoldering ruins of
ued to throw off a
riving choppers sca
begun to circle abov
by the brutal attack

In charge of the
Webster, a youth
who'd paid his du
months of America'
With no survivors
pened, Webster was
overview of the situ
conclusions.

There were a fev
scattered on the gr
tracks in the dirt s
proached the disabl
the wilderness.

"I want a coupl
tain barked to the n
their Iroquois. He

base with a
divided the
charged with
with searchin
light on the

Although
its side and
were tilted a
upright and
men warily
other cars ar
the Smallboy
nestled secur
ilarly, the la
been tamper
men to come
Webster with
taken.

"Damn!"
possible cons
through the
with the base
told the new
thets of his

"At least
elly voice cr
plutonium an
anything but

"I don't k
me they mig
ket. Lot of
technology a

'em apart and figure out how to make 'em, then put in their own plutonium and—"

"Yeah, yeah, all right," Hedge conceded. "And we might be in for some kind of heavy-duty blackmail from some nut-case maniacs. It's a goddamn mess any way you slice it. You said there are no survivors?"

"Not that we can see, sir."

"Meaning what?"

"Well, sir," Webster said, "bad as that barracks car was hit, we're going to have a hard time counting bodies. Whoever did this might have taken some hostages."

"Or maybe the traitorous bastards that helped set this up from the inside might have gone off with the raiders."

"It's a possibility, sir."

There was an audible groan from Hedge, then he said, "We better clamp a tight lid on this mess before the press gets a whiff or there's going to be hell to pay. Understood?"

"Loud and clear, sir."

The two officers signed off and Webster walked away from the chopper, letting the severity of the situation sink in as he approached the growing heap of bodies next to the train. He recognized some of the less disfigured fatalities, good men he'd come to know over the four years he'd been stationed at Fort Shaw. Some of them had wives and children. He'd been an usher at PFC W. C. Amst's wedding only last summer, and now he was staring at the young man's mutilated body sprawled in a lifeless heap before him. There was no trace yet of either Lieutenant Texico or Colonel Washgan, but Webster was certain of their loyalty and felt a pang of sick grief at the thought that they were probably lost in the carnage of the barracks car. Ashes to ashes. Remember, man, dust thou art, and unto dust thou shalt return.

"Sir?"

Webster turned to face one of the pilots, who'd just come over from his chopper. "We just got a report from the search party."

"And...?"

"They traced the tracks to Owyhee River and found a couple Forestry Service trucks ditched in the water."

"Ditched?"

"Afraid so, sir. No tracks on the other side. They must have had a boat waiting or something. We're checking up- and downstream and then we'll try the lake, but it doesn't look promising."

"Shit!" Webster waved the other men away. His nerves were going wild on him and he needed a few moments alone to rein them back under control. Whoever had masterminded the train attack was a formidable opponent, and the stakes were rising each moment they remained at large. Unless they were found and stopped, the enemy might eventually have at its disposal a means of destruction that would make the Cessna's kamikaze run look like child's play.

Chasing its shadow across the color-drenched Virginia countryside, the Hughes 500-D helicopter purred contentedly under the control of Jack Grimaldi, crackerjack pilot for one of the nation's foremost sources of covert manpower. In the employ of Stony Man Farm, a top-secret installation nestled in the lush expanse of Shenandoah Valley, Grimaldi put in flight time both abroad and at home. Overseas, he was usually at the service of either Stony Man One, Mack Bolan, or the five-man antiterrorist unit known as Phoenix Force. Today he was shuttling Carl Lyons and Pol Blancanales, two-thirds of Able Team, the domestic branch of the Stony Man operations groups, as well as Hal Brognola, the outfit's main strategist and its liaison with Washington.

The men were on their way back from the capital, having just attended a top-level, confidential meeting concerned with the recent incident in the Oregon wilderness. In the wake of disclosures that had been part of the briefing, the men were grim-faced and had barely spoken since leaving Washington. Lyons finally broke the silence.

"I'm beginning to understand how Sisyphus felt," he murmured, running callused fingers through his short blond hair. Blue-eyed and square-jawed, Lyons had the look of a somewhat aging California surf bum, but although he hailed from L.A., the man's taste for thrills seldom took him to the beach and his life was dedicated less to catching the perfect wave than riding roughshod over any number of sociopaths terrorizing his country in the name of their assorted causes.

"Sisyphus?" Brognola raised a bushy eyebrow and glanced to the back seat, where Lyons sat next to Blancanales. "Aren't we getting a little heady, Ironman?"

"Hey, you're the one who's always on our butts to keep our minds as much in shape as our bodies, chief," Lyons taunted back. "I've been brushing up on my mythology, okay? This Sisyphus guy had to put up with the same kind of futile shit as us. Some things never change."

"Maybe so," Blancanales interjected with a grin, "but do you really have to compare us with someone who's first name was Sissy?"

"Ha-ha, you're a real comedian, Pol," Lyons drawled, planting an elbow in his cohort's side. "Let me return the favor and tickle *your* ribs a little, too."

The two men sparred briefly, deliberately pulling their punches since they were more concerned with letting off steam than doing any harm. With 380 pounds of war-trained muscle between them, the chopper would have been the loser if the men had been fighting in earnest. As it was, Grimaldi had to jockey the controls to keep the small aircraft stable.

"Hey, you brats keep fighting in the back seat and it's to bed without dinner for both of you," the Italian pilot snapped, putting a little parental bite into his words even though he was roughly the same age as the others—pushing forty and not too thrilled about it.

Lyons and Blancanales calmed down after Grimaldi banked the Hughes sharply to his right, dipping perilously close to Jenkins Gap at the north end of the Blue Ridge Mountains. They were now more than halfway back to the Farm.

Lyons's allusion to Sisyphus had been an appropriate one, considering the endless battle Able Team found itself embroiled in. Like that mythological antihero whose massive boulder rolled back downhill within moments after he'd labored long and hard to move it up a steep incline, it seemed that whenever Able Team managed to eliminate a dire threat in one part of the country, more hell broke loose elsewhere. As an example, a recent assignment in Nashville, where they'd gone head-to-head with a terrorist group headed by a renegade KGB agent, Sergei Karanov, had come on the heels of a small-scale war waged in the isolated hills of San Diego County, where a Soviet-backed religious commune had used disciples as human guinea pigs in mind-control experiments directed toward infiltrating naval facilities in San Diego harbor.

On and on the relentless chain of action and reaction extended, back to the day, more than half a decade ago, when widespread global villainy had reached such proportions that the call had gone out for additional manpower to supplement those efforts already being undertaken by the likes of Delta Force, the SEALs and the Green Berets. All four men in the Hughes 500-D had seen more than their share of humanity's underbelly in the intervening years, and the enemy had a thousand faces. International terrorists, drug-dealing desperadoes, mob hit men, wandering psychopaths—Able Team had faced them all, and despite enough battle scars and wounds to have disabled an army of lesser men, the Team had lived to tell the tale, and weary though they were, when the next emergency arose, the men would throw themselves into the fray once again with the same selfless abandon that had pulled them through the fire so many times before.

"Anybody want to lay bets on who's behind this shit in Oregon?" Lyons asked as they found themselves entering Shenandoah Valley, a long, deep gash in the Blue Ridge Mountains rightly designated as a national park. "I've got forty bucks says it's Russkies."

"No way," Blancanales said. "Hell, they've got enough warheads of their own without having to go to all the trouble of nabbing some of ours. I'll go forty on Libya."

Brognola shook his head contemptuously. "I can't believe what I'm hearing. Wagering on something of this nature hardly seems appropriate."

"Oh yeah?" Lyons countered. "Well, who was it that got us bucks for a gymnasium at the Farm by betting the Secret Service we could get past them and pretend to shoot the President? Huh, chief? Wanna answer that one?"

Brognola blushed slightly as he withdrew a Honduran cigar from his coat and fiddled absently with its ring band. "I guess you got me there, Carl. Guilty as charged."

"I'll put money on an inside job. Killer moles," Grimaldi said.

"Oh, very well." Brognola sighed. "I'll play along and say it's some new domestic group looking to become a reckoning force."

"That should cover most bases," Lyons said.

Wagering completed, the men were interrupted by the crackling of the chopper's radio speakers. It was Aaron Kurtzman, Stony Man's burly communications wizard, calling from the Farm. After making the usual security clearances, he asked Grimaldi, "How's your fuel situation, Jack?"

Grimaldi eyed his control gauges. "Plenty enough to get us home."

"Enough to get you upstate?"

"I don't know, probably. Why?"

"Got a problem up in Cumberland," Kurtzman confided. "Seems there's plutonium missing from the Nuclear Research Center up there."

"How much?" Brognola cut in.

"Enough," Kurtzman said. There was no need to elaborate.

Grimaldi yanked back on his pitch stick and the Hughes tilted upward, heading out of the valley and turning north. "We're on our way," he told Kurtzman.

WHILE HIS PARTNERS were answering the call to Cumberland, Able Team's third member, Gadgets Schwarz, was on the other side of the continent, paying a rare visit to Pasadena, his hometown. The occasion was a bittersweet one, brought about by the most recent earthquake to have rattled its way along

the West Coast. Although the tremor had only regis-
tered at a relatively unthreatening 4.3 on the Richter
scale, its epicenter had been in nearby Highland Park,
and the brunt of the aftershocks had radiated north-
ward through the Pasadena area, jostling expensive
homes and older structures erected prior to the enact-
ment of building codes designed to minimize structural damage in the event of quakes. Of the latter
buildings, the hardest hit had been Wheaton Street
High School, which had already suffered tangible
foundation damage in the Whittier trembler of 1987.
Structural engineers had examined the school after the
latest shake and declared it unfit for further use. When
orders to have the building demolished were issued,
word had gone out through the Wheaton High Alumni Association, and Schwarz was one of more than
five thousand former students who showed up for the
scheduled demolition.

Never too keen on nostalgia and a firm believer in
Satchel Paige's dictum, "Don't look back," Schwarz
had made it a point to skip every announced class re-
union since his graduation more than twenty years
ago. High School hadn't held much in the way of
pleasant memories for Schwarz, whose academic
leanings and adolescent gangliness had earned him the
derisive nicknames of Egghead, Four Eyes and
Munster, the latter based on the fact that his first
name, Hermann, was the same as that of the clumsy
monster character played by Fred Gwynn on the pop-
ular TV series. However, the announcement of the
demolition had reached him at the same time as he'd
been preparing to visit Southern California on busi-

ness, and on a whim he'd decided to pay his respects to the dying building.

Within minutes of putting on a name tag that listed his graduating year and starting to mingle with the other alumni, Schwarz was glad he had come. He hadn't grown any taller than his five-foot-ten height at the time of his graduation, but he'd put on forty-five pounds to bring his weight up to an imposing 170, and a steady exercise regimen and life of activity dating back to his years of service in Vietnam had honed his coordination and put to rest any semblance of the awkwardness that had made him the butt of so many teenage jokes. His new nickname of Gadgets was one he was comfortable with; it was a flattering tribute to the technological skills he'd mastered over the years. As he walked proudly and confidently among his former classmates, he couldn't help but gloat inwardly at what had become of his old high school nemeses. A lot of the football jocks and self-envisioned ladies' men were now balding and potbellied, looking worn-out from their nine-to-five suburban grinds. He could barely suppress a laugh at the sight of Dave Bing, an inveterate wiseass and Schwarz's ultimate tormentor at Wheaton, passing around business cards in hopes of increasing sales at his used-car lot in neighboring Burbank. And as for the girls who years ago had spurned him as the class nerd, many were now dowdy-looking hausfraus wearing the sad expression of women whose lives had wound up parked in a dead end of mediocrity.

Then there was Rona Lynne.

She had been the closest thing Schwarz had to a girlfriend in high school. Rona had been the female bookworm of the class and salutatorian to Schwarz's valedictorian. Both teased by their contemporaries, Gadgets and Rona had been bound together in a platonic alliance, cementing their friendship over study sessions and taking trips to case out the facilities at Cal Tech or tour electronics manufacturing plants while other students were building class floats and partying at the local burger hangout. Back then she'd dressed to suit her reputation, wearing horn-rimmed glasses, pulled-back hair and bulky, unflattering sweaters. But over the years she'd transformed herself into something of a knockout, and Schwarz had to do a double take when he glanced at her name tag. Now Rona was dressed in a stylish Anne Klein II ensemble, and her reddish hair was layered with a light perm that complemented her well-sculptured features. Tinted contacts had turned her brown eyes blue.

"Rona?" Schwarz said, still staring at the woman with disbelief.

She was equally stunned at the sight of him. "Hermann?" she gasped, glancing up from his name tag. "Is that really you?"

Schwarz grinned. "Sure is. Long time no see, as they say."

"They've been saying it all day here." Rona laughed. She looked Gadgets over again. "The years have certainly treated you well. You look great."

"Same for you, Rona," Schwarz said. "I'm a little confused, though. Your name tag says you still go by Lynne, but you've got a wedding ring."

"Married five years," Rona said, glancing down at the ring finger on her hand. A dark look came over her face briefly, then gave way to a faint smile. "Kept my maiden name, though. Picked up a little feminism along the way, you know."

"Who's the lucky guy? Anybody I know?"

"Maybe. Mel Bronson. He was a couple years ahead of us."

Schwarz thought back and nodded. "Football player, right? Homecoming king when we were sophomores."

"That's him," Rona said.

"Well, it sure looks like marriage agrees with you," Schwarz said.

Rona sighed and the troubled look returned. "Actually, we're separated right now."

"Oops, sorry," Schwarz said. "Next topic."

Rona forced a short laugh. They broke away from the rest of the throng and spent the better part of the next half hour catching up on each other.

Although the relative confidentiality of his job precluded any mention of Able Team, Schwarz was able to tell her about his years in Nam, his love of computers and some of the places he'd been to as a technology research analyst for an East-Coast-based think tank. In a way, he wasn't straying too far from the truth, although his business trips for Able Team had a tendency to be concerned less with thinking and research than with the noncerebral laying one's life on the line in a head-on collision with the world's vermin.

Rona explained that she'd gone on to school at Cal Tech and had become heavily involved in earthquake studies based out of the Institute. In particular, she was currently part of a controversial project looking into the almost virgin territory of earthquake control.

In collaboration with the United States Geological Survey and a state-of-the-art monitoring station in Ventura County, Rona's team was investigating the possibilities of using a controlled combination of advanced chemical laser technology and strategically placed nuclear charges to relieve frictional stress points created by grinding tectonic plates along California's numerous unstable fault lines.

"That's incredible," Schwarz exclaimed once Rona had finished describing her job.

"How so?" she asked.

"Well," Schwarz explained, "one of the reasons I'm in town is because a guy I work with is here looking into that project on behalf of the Pentagon."

He was referring to John "Cowboy" Kissinger, armorer and weaponsmith for the Stony Man Operations Group and also an engineering graduate from Ohio State and MIT. Of course, Kissinger was working only partly on behalf of the Pentagon, whose funded SDI laser research had played an indirect but major part in the earthquake control strategies. In his capacity as guardian of the Farm's arsenal, Kissinger was always on the lookout for innovations that might help both Able Team and Phoenix Force in their endless war against terrorism. Already Cowboy had brought in such newfangled weapons as the remote-controlled FOG-M missile system, and he was intrigued by the possibilities of putting lasers to use as an antiterrorist tool. While Schwarz and Rona Lynne were in Pasadena to witness the demolition of Wheaton High, Kissinger was across town, meeting with Rona's fellow workers and other individuals committed to the vital cause of reducing the risk of a major earthquake's causing widespread death and destruction to the nation's most populous state.

"Maybe you'd like to meet him," Schwarz suggested to Rona. "I'll be in touch with him at some get-together at the Pacific Asia Museum a little later on."

"Oh, of course," Rona said. "That's being put on by our people for the Orient Seismological Collective. I planned on being there myself."

"Could I escort you there?" Schwarz asked. "I understand there's a dinner afterward."

"Thanks, I'd like that," Rona said.

They were interrupted by the head of the alumni association, a gray-haired, bespectacled member of the class of '53. Speaking over a muffled public-address system, he announced that the demolition would be taking place shortly. But before that big event, he introduced a member of the first graduating class from Wheaton, beginning what turned out to be another half hour's worth of speeches from other alumni and administrators fondly recalling the school's finer moments. There was a decidedly melancholy tone to all of the speeches, rendered with the somberness of eulogies, and even Schwarz felt a tug in his throat by the time the last speaker had concluded his remarks with a call for everyone to join him in singing the school song. It was years since Schwarz had had cause to voice the lyrics, but the words were emblazoned in his memory, squeezed in with those few fond recollections of his Wheaton days. He and Rona sang along with the five thousand other voices raised in unison, and tears flowed freely down many a saddened face by the time the last verse had been repeated a second time.

Then, as directed, there was a minute of silence as the throng looked past a waist-high restraining fence surrounding the school and stared at the tall brownstone building that showed few outward signs of its structural instability. Schwarz recalled a few more memories of times spent inside those hallowed halls. Then, drawing in a deep breath, he bade the school farewell.

Seconds later, a series of four explosions rocked the building's foundations. One moment the structure was standing, aged but dignified in the late-morning sun; the next it was crumbling in on itself in a shower of falling brick and plaster. The explosives had been so expertly placed and detonated that the entire building was leveled in a matter of seconds, with not so much as a stray brick or shard of glass flying more than a few feet away from the monstrous heap of rubble that emerged into view as the cloud of raised dust began to settle.

It was a stunning, mesmerizing sight, and some time passed before the onlookers recovered from their shock and began to speak to one another in hushed tones. There were loud sobs and many people embraced one another, moved as deeply as if they had just witnessed the body of a loved one being lowered into the ground at a funeral ceremony.

Rona and Gadgets walked off together, momentarily lost in their own thoughts. "That was something," Gadgets said, finally breaking the silence.

"I'll say," Rona admitted. However, she was thinking less in terms of nostalgia and more about the hard realities behind the demolition. "Hard to believe that a strong quake could have brought it down just as quickly."

"You're kidding, right?" Schwarz said.

"I wish," she told him. "I saw the evaluations and they figured that even another 6.1 quake could have done the job if the land rolled the wrong way."

"Pretty scary."

"The really scary thing is that there are still thousands of unreinforced buildings throughout the state that could come down like that when the big one hits," Rona said. "That's why we're going to such efforts to try to tame the faults."

Schwarz glanced back over his shoulder at the mound of fallen bricks, letting out a low whisper. "I knew there was a reason that I moved back East."

2

Cumberland, the governing seat of Maryland's gun-shaped Allegheny County, sat on the banks of the Potomac River, a short row from West Virginia. Originally called Fort Cumberland in the late eighteenth century when it served as military headquarters for General Edward Braddock and Lieutenant George Washington during the French and Indian Wars, the city had a rich historical legacy. It was a history highlighted by the boomtown years before the twentieth century. Back then it was coal, iron and steel—mainstay elements wrested from the earth in the name of the Industrial Revolution—that paved the way for wealth and growth in the area. Washington Street still boasted the numerous Federal and Georgian Revival mansions that mining and rail barons had erected in tribute to prosperity gleaned off the land.

In recent years, however, the nouveau riche of Cumberland had drawn their income from decidedly more contemporary enterprises. Though the traditional industries still held their ground to some extent, a close look at any of the more prosperous suburbs revealed that the professional background of the newer homeowners leaned more toward nuclear physics, engineering and computer technology. The reason for the change could be found by taking a drive through the area and noting the signs posted outside some of the buildings and industrial complexes that had appeared in the past three decades. Places like Eastern Dynamics, Potomac Semiconductors, Allegheny Computer Systems and Cumberland Nuclear Research Center. Although these and related industries were separately owned, they often dipped into the same talent pool and catered to the same clientele, primarily the Defense Department and Atomic Energy Commission. As Cumberland headed toward the twenty-first century, it had made its pact with the future and was fast becoming a major center for both nuclear studies and weapons development. For instance, Eastern Dynamics was under contract for development of the guidance systems for the XT-22 missile, while the Cumberland Nuclear Research Center's fast breeder reactors were responsible for converting uranium fuel into the plutonium-239 that eventually would find itself inside the XT-22 warheads.

The latter facility was located on the outskirts of town, on a twelve-acre parcel of land surrounded by a high, spike-topped, wrought-iron fence and guarded by a twenty-seven man security force. There was a monstrous helipad in the middle of the complex, and when Jack Grimaldi brought down the Hughes 500-D, he couldn't help but notice four refurbished Hueys resting on the far edge of the tarmac.

"Looks like they're ready for an evacuation," he said as he cut power on his chopper's twenty-six-foot rotors.

"They're *always* ready for evacuation," Brognola said as he unfastened his seat belt and prepared to disembark. "Standard precaution when you're dealing with the kind of things these folks have on their hands...."

"Yeah, I guess so."

Once Grimaldi and Brognola were out, Lyons and Blancanales emerged and all four men followed a security escort into the nearest building, a three-story futuristic complex that housed the Center's administrative facilities. They were led to a windowless ground-floor meeting room with a wraparound wall mural depicting a panoramic view of the grounds.

"Help yourself to refreshments," their escort told them. "The boss will be with you shortly."

"Interesting touch," Blancanales said, taking a closer look at the painting. "Almost makes it feel like we're in the penthouse."

"Probably the idea, no doubt." Lyons snorted. "I'll bet some junior executive thought it up as part of a pride-on-the-job campaign."

"Since you're so impressed, maybe we should do the same thing at our conference room back at the Farm," Brognola suggested.

"That's okay, chief. Get the gym put up and we'll have all the morale boost we need."

Lyons went over to the corner of the room, where a five-gallon urn of coffee rested on a table along with Styrofoam cups, packets of nondairy creamer and a pastry basket heaped high with day-old breakfast rolls. Lyons filled a cup with coffee and dunked a Danish into it before taking his first bite. "Edible," he declared. "Just barely."

Blancanales and Brognola followed suit. Several moments later they were joined by a gruff-looking man in his late fifties, wearing a navy-colored uniform and carrying a manila file and a pint-size mug already filled with steaming coffee. From the weary look in his hazel eyes and the dark circles under them, it seemed a safe bet that the coffee was taking the place of lost sleep. He introduced himself as Joseph Corriter, head of Center security.

"Thanks for coming on such short notice," Corriter told his guests after introductions were completed. "Please have a seat."

The other men carried their snacks over to a small conference table in the middle of the room, and sat down. Corriter joined them after helping himself to the last of the rolls, muttering how it was the first solid food he'd had since dawn. He asked Brognola how much preliminary information Able Team had been given.

"Just that you're missing some plutonium," Brognola said. "That's all we needed to know to figure this rated top priority."

"Good, I'm glad." Corriter swallowed his roll in three quick bites and washed it down with coffee, then opened his file and shook his head miserably. "Five, ten years ago I would have been too goddamn proud and territorial to put up with outsiders sniffing around my turf, but on this one I know we can use all the help we can get. We've already called in DOE people and the FBI, so they've got a head start on you. But their authority extends only so far, and I've been told that you have certain, shall we say, additional latitude as far as what you can do...."

Lyons leaned forward in his seat and told Corriter impatiently, "We already know we're the pit bulls of the trade, so how about if we get down to basics, okay?"

Corriter eyed Lyons blandly and looked as if he were about to say something. He caught himself, however, and turned his attention back to Brognola. "As part of our regular security routine, we conduct full-scale inventories every five days. Parts, fuel, incoming and outgoing materials—the whole works. It's usually been just going through the motions, because this is a tightly run ship and nothing of much significance has ever turned up missing."

"Until now," Blancanales put in.

"Yes, until this morning." Corriter withdrew a map of the Center facilities and laid it out so the other four men could see where he was pointing. "Here's the reactor, and next to it's the sealing-and-shipment plant. The plutonium had to have been taken from either of these two places, and at some point during the past four days. We suspect it happened last Friday."

"Why's that?"

Corriter finished his coffee, then took two photographs clipped to computer printouts and passed them to Brognola before going to the urn for a refill. "These two men were on graveyard shift Friday and neither of them reported to work this morning after having the weekend off. Both had access and opportunity to have pulled a heist."

"Who are they?" Brognola asked, glancing at the photos, which looked to be standard head shots taken for security name tags.

"The older man's Dr. Robert Yurvi," Corriter explained. "Romanian physicist. Defected to the West fifteen years ago. He's been senior scientist on the breeder reactor team since '84. Genius on the job, they say. Photographic memory, quick with figures. Has an engineering degree, too, so he knows nuts and bolts as well as theory. A real loner, though. Has a cheap apartment just down the block. No one has seen him since early Saturday morning."

"Sounds like maybe he didn't completely defect after all," Lyons speculated once the file information reached him. He looked at the photo of Yurvi, then of the second man. "And this guy was security, right?"

Corriter nodded. "Montgomery Landlicott. Been with us since '84, too. Hired on a month after Yurvi came here, as a matter of fact."

"What a coincidence," Blancanales said.

"Right," Corriter agreed. "Just like with Yurvi, last anyone saw of Landlicott was Saturday morning. A neighbor saw him put a suitcase and some kind of heavy box in the trunk of his Buick and drive off."

"And what's his background?" Brognola asked. "Anything to link him with Yurvi?"

Corriter ran his hand through his salt-and-pepper hair, then sighed as he nodded his head. "Landlicott's native-born. Illinois. But he's got family on his mother's side back in Romania. We haven't been able to trace connections to Yurvi, but the relatives live in Bucharest and that's where Yurvi was based before he defected."

Brognola digested the information and rose from the table, pacing back and forth as he mulled over a course of action. "And you obviously have no leads on where either of them might have gone."

"Only that Landlicott's Buick was traced to a private airfield out near Frostburg," Corriter said. "Neither he nor Yurvi own any planes there and nobody recalls seeing them. Had disguises, no doubt."

"We can get Kurtzman to run a check on all the planes and owners," Blancanales ventured, knowing that Stony Man's communications officer was as adept with his computers as magicians were with their wands. Given even the barest of raw information to work with, Kurtzman could be off and running, fingers on his keyboards, effortlessly accessing whatever data banks he felt might yield another clue or tidbit, regardless of whatever so-called anti-hacking measures might have been taken to prevent outsiders from tapping into such information.

"I assume the FBI's covered ground as far as conducting interviews with your personnel?" Brognola said.

"Sure have." Corriter unclipped a business card from the file in front of him and handed it to the Stony Man chief. "Here's the guy heading things up for them. Stan Turdrin. He's at the Holiday Inn."

"Good. We'll touch base with him and make sure we aren't treading the same water. Obviously we don't want to waste any time on this." Brognola sat back down and drummed his fingertips lightly on the tabletop, then continued, "This plutonium. Any chance it could be matched up with those XT-22 warheads that got lifted in Oregon?"

"I'm afraid so," Corriter said. "What's more, Yurvi also did some consulting across town at Eastern Dynamics. They make the guidance systems for the XT-22. No question but that he knows that warhead inside and out."

Lyons coughed to get his cohort's attention. "Well, if this Yurvi's still loyal to his roots, then the odds are his strings are being pulled by Russia. Looks like I'm gonna win our little bet, guys."

HANNAS-MA YANG HAD BEEN driving almost nonstop for the past eight hours and the road fatigue was beginning to wear on him. He yawned, then swallowed a methamphetamine tablet in hopes of giving himself another chemical jolt to get him through this final leg of the Yellow River Brigade's flight from the Harney Basin.

So far everything had gone according to plan. After reaching the Owyhee River in the two Forestry Service trucks, the men had changed from their uniforms into casual clothes and transferred their cargo of stolen XT-22s to a pair of lightweight speedboats that had swiftly carried them to their next rendezvous point, a sheltered cove along the northwest banks of Lake Owyhee, a forty-mile-long watercourse near the Oregon–Idaho border. From there they had made one final transfer into a battered, sixteen-year-old Winnebago. Like the Forestry Service trucks and the speedboats, the mobile home had been secured in trade as part of the Brigade's opium dealings with both Nevada organized crime figures and independent dealers in Northern California.

From Lake Owyhee, the men had quickly driven up to Ontario, then over into Idaho and down Interstate 80 until it linked up with Route 93 south, which had taken them into Nevada. It was a meandering detour to their intended destination, but Hannas-ma Yang had plotted the way deliberately, knowing that by crossing as many county and state lines as possible, they would increase the odds against local law enforcement agencies tracking their moves.

While Hannas-ma drove and his twenty-year-old brother, Jon, rode shotgun beside him, the other men were in back, either sleeping or fidgeting nervously in their seats, M-14s across their laps. The man wounded in the raid lay in a fold-down bed, bleeding through his dressing and tossing as a fever burned through him. A comrade sitting near the bed readied an opium syringe and gave the injured man an injection. Within moments the man calmed visibly, closing his eyes and focusing on matters other than his pain.

Two other terrorists were monitoring CB and shortwave radios in hopes of keeping abreast of any official bulletins regarding the raid and the search for its perpetrators. Thus far there had been no news, which in the case of the Brigade, was good news. It seemed a safe guess that with no survivors left behind at the immobilized train, the authorities had no descriptions of the raiders to go on...not that any such descriptions would have been accurate, for the men had changed clothes and those who had darkened their skins had long since rubbed off the artificial pigment.

Still, whenever a highway patrol car was spotted on the road or a police chopper droned overhead, there would be a tense hush inside the rolling motor home. The Brigade was bound by oath to refuse capture, and if need be, all were prepared to die on the highway, riddling as many motorists and lawmen as possible before they themselves were cut down. In each instance, however, the police vehicles passed by and moved on without incident, their drivers preoccupied with the apprehension of speeders.

Ironically, the final stretch of the band's circuitous flight took them past the Nellis Air Force Range and Nuclear Testing Site northwest of Las Vegas. This was where the United States Atomic Energy Commission staged the majority of its underground nuclear tests, including those for XT-22s similar to those concealed in storage compartments of the Winnebago.

The sun was setting behind the White Mountains of Inyo National Forest when Hannas-ma Yang crossed yet another state line and entered California. The men paused to refuel the Winnebago and grab some fast food at a truck stop in Oasis, then proceeded west past Deep Springs, across the northernmost stretch of Eureka Valley and up through Westgard Pass.

"A long day, Brother, yes?" Jon said as he watched stars come out in the California night, looking like pinprick holes through which the light of another universe shone.

Hannas-ma nodded. "And a successful one. Not that I had any doubts."

Jon laughed. "Hah! You may be able to fool the others, but not me."

"I had concern, not doubts," Hannas-ma insisted. "There is a difference."

"Whatever you say, Brother. What's important is that now we are finally on our way to making an impact."

"Exactly," the older brother responded. "From this day onward, the Yellow River Brigade is no longer a small voice in the wilderness. Now when we act, people will take notice."

"We will be like the American's E. F. Hutton," Jon chuckled. "When we talk, people will listen."

"Of course, with the XT-22s doing our talking, it might be too loud for anyone to hear anything else."

Jon laughed. "True, Brother. True."

Clearing Westgard Pass, the Winnebago started downhill. Owens Valley lay below them, bisected by the gleaming water of the Los Angeles Aqueduct and by Highway 395, the main thoroughfare of the region, which was alive with the roving headlights of nighttime traffic.

"Are we almost there?" one of the men in the back of the motor home called out.

"Yes," Hannas-ma Yang replied as he noted a sign announcing their proximity to Big Pine. "Why?"

"Because Deng has died," the man reported solemnly, glancing at the bleeding man on the bed. He reached out and closed the victim's vacant-staring eyes.

Hannas-ma's knuckles whitened on the steering wheel and he muttered a curse in his native tongue, then assured his comrades, "We will see to it that he did not die in vain."

3

California's fragile land mass was only part of a much larger earthquake-prone area known among seismologists as the dreaded Ring of Fire. Running along the entire west coast of South, Central and North America, the Ring extended across the Aleutians and then south through Japan and the Philippines, through New Zealand, and back across the Pacific to complete the circle in Chile. There was almost universal agreement that the friction buildup between the shifting tectonic plates bordering this region was more volatile than anywhere else on earth, and that recurring cataclysmic tremors were a grim inevitability.

Such being the case, in recent years there had been a great deal of cooperation between earthquake scientists working within the Ring, and the hope was that the collaboration effort might help reduce losses of life and property during shakes, particularly in those countries that had yet to adopt stringent building codes and other prescriptive measures. The most promising development in this area had been the recent creation of a team of Chinese, Philippine and Japanese scientists, who had decided to pool their quake study resources and subsequently send a dele-

gation to the United States for an exchange of ideas
and technologies.

As fate would have it, the Orient Seismological
Collective had set up its headquarters in Taipei at the
same time Able Team's erstwhile female associate,
Lao Ti, had moved to that city to tend to her ailing
mother. Although Lao, of Vietnamese and Mon-
golian extraction, had originally joined up with the
Stony Man operation as a technical assistant to Aaron
Kurtzman, she had done her share of time in the
trenches, more than holding her own as she fought
alongside the men of Able Team. Familiar with a di-
verse range of firearms and deadly proficient in the
martial arts, the petite female dynamo had been an
invaluable ally up to the time of her near-death in
Cincinnati the previous winter, when she had been
gunned down while helping Able Team protect a
mobster-turned-informant marked for execution by
his former syndicate cronies.

After successfully nursing both her mother and
herself back to health, Lao Ti had been deliberating as
to what she wanted to do with her life when she heard
that the OSC was seeking an English-speaking computer expert who could double as part of the liaison
team that would be sent to America. She applied for
the job and so impressed her interviewers that she was
hired on the spot. During the ensuing eight months she
had applied herself with intense dedication and concentration, honing her skills to the point that she became a key player on the OSC's team bound for the
United States.

And now she was back in the States. Although the
cultural differences were significant, in many ways Lao

Ti felt as if she'd never left. The country was like a second home to her, and being there felt right, although one thing was missing. She felt a need to get back in touch with her old friends and acquaintances, especially those from Stony Man Farm. When she put through a call to Virginia, using her personalized code and employing the necessary security diversions, she was happily surprised to learn from Aaron Kurtzman that not only were two of her friends in Southern California, but they were both there in part because of Stony Man's tactical interest in United States–OSC quake-control weapons development. She wasn't sure how she'd missed them during the day's earlier activities, and after ending the call to Kurtzman, she was doubly determined to track down Gadgets Schwarz and Cowboy Kissinger, even if it meant canvasing all of Pasadena on foot. Fortunately, she knew that such drastic measures would not be necessary, as that evening a reception was being held for quake personnel in the conference room of the Pacific Asia Museum on North Los Robles, followed by a banquet dinner down the block at the Oriental Gardens Restaurant. She decided to start her search at the museum.

Short and trim, Lao Ti had lost some of the sculptured musculature she had meticulously maintained prior to being wounded, but diligent physical therapy had helped her to overcome what the doctors had predicted would be a lifelong limp caused by the proximity of bullet wounds to her spine. Wearing a tailored pantsuit and her now customary flats, Lao Ti mingled amid the guests gathered in the museum's reception area, keeping an eye open for Schwarz and Kissinger. She exchanged pleasantries with her colleagues and engaged in several brief conversations with her American hosts about the earlier tour of the facilities where the controversial quake-control laser and particle-beam system were being developed. Lao Ti held the position that, if and when properly executed, any major breakthrough in the control technology should rate as highly as any advances generated by the space programs of the superpowers. In fact, she said, the day that a control device developed jointly by the United States and the Orient Seismological Collective was successfully used to prevent an anticipated quake should go down in the history books as being as important as the day man first walked on the moon. At this gathering there were few who would have disagreed with her.

Lao Ti had been in the room for more than forty-five minutes before she finally spotted one of the men she was looking for. John Kissinger was standing near the hors d'oeuvres table, talking with a man Lao Ti recognized as part of the U.S. quake-control weapons team. At six-foot-two and two hundred pounds, Kissinger was the biggest of the Stony Men, and he'd earned his nickname of Cowboy for the way he'd recklessly put that linebacker's body into the fray while a frontline man with the Drug Enforcement Administration in the late seventies. He still looked more than capable of busting a few heads.

"I think the particle-beam system has more potential on this front than lasers," Kissinger was telling the other man as Lao Ti wandered within earshot. "It's just a matter of honing down the control mechanisms so you can use it with greater accuracy."

The other man was half a head shorter than Kissinger but the same weight, much of it centered around his ample midsection. He smiled indulgently at Kissinger's remark. "Is this the Pentagon speaking now or just you personally?"

"Trust me," Lao Ti said, entering the conversation. "John Kissinger only speaks for himself."

Kissinger turned to his left and an expression of surprise unfolded across his face as he recognized Lao Ti. She'd changed her hairstyle since the last time he'd seen her, letting her dark hair cascade to her shoulders and wearing her bangs proportionately longer.

"Lao Ti!"

"Hello, Cowboy," she said, smiling. "Small world, isn't it?"

"I'll say." Kissinger handled introductions between Lao Ti and the other man, who then excused himself to have another go at the hors d'oeuvres. Cowboy gave Lao Ti another once-over, then shook his head, pleasantly amazed. "Damn, it's great to see you looking so good, Lao," he told her. "I have to admit, we were all a little worried about you when you left for Taipei."

"So was I," Lao Ti confessed. "But you know what they say. Can't keep a good woman down." She went on to explain her reasons for being in Pasadena and how she'd known she'd find him in town. "Where's Gadgets?" she finally asked.

"You just missed him," Kissinger said. "He was here for just a few minutes with an old friend who's part of the Cal Tech team. They went over to Oriental Gardens already to meet some of her people. What say we join them?"

"Love to," Lao Ti said.

On their way out of the museum, the two of them paused to view a few art pieces on display in the main hallway.

"This one's my favorite," she said, pointing to a delicately carved Oriental statue of rose-colored ivory mounted on a pedestal near the service elevator. Atop a round, squat, foot-high tower were a dozen gargoyles, each leaning outward at equidistant points on the circular surface, like marks on a clock. Their heads hung down slightly, and their jaws were partially opened, holding small balls of white ivory. Several inches below each figure was a lavishly carved cup roughly the same size as the balls.

"One of the first quake measurers," Lao Ti explained as she pointed to the gargoyles. "In theory, whichever monster dropped its ball during a tremor would point out the direction the shake was coming from. Not exactly state of the art, but not bad for eight hundred years ago, either."

"Pretty ingenious, all right." As they went outside and headed for his rented Chrysler, Cowboy added, "But isn't it true that they still use some primitive methods back in the Orient? Stuff like watching animal behavior and doing radon readings from water wells?"

Lao Ti nodded. "A lot of people scoff at that and it's not always foolproof, but there've been more than a few times when those kind of techniques have saved a lot of lives."

As they left the parking lot and started down the road toward Oriental Gardens, Lao Ti cited an example in China during the mid-seventies, when geologists relying primarily on crude methodologies predicted that a quake reaching 5.5 to 6.0 on the Richter scale would strike within six months in the vicinity of Haicheng in the Liaoning province. A month later the first small tremors came, and further measurements prompted an evacuation of densely populated Haicheng less than ten hours before a 7.3 shaker devastated the city. Thanks to the prediction and evacuation, the death toll had been held down to a handful rather than the more than one hundred thousand fatalities experts claimed would have occurred otherwise.

"That's pretty impressive," Kissinger murmured as he drove down Los Robles. "By the same token, though, haven't there been false alarms?"

"Yes, but—"

"Well, can you imagine what would happen out here if the governor ordered L.A. evacuated because of a prediction, only to have nothing happen? It'd be chaos. People would want his head for being such an alarmist."

Lao Ti countered, "Well, suppose he ignored a prediction because he didn't want to risk egg on his face and then a quake *did* hit L.A. without warning. You know the projections on that."

Kissinger nodded. Even with modernized construction techniques, it had been estimated that a mega-quake striking Los Angeles at six in the morning would kill up to three thousand people, and if the same tremor occurred during peak traffic periods the toll could be expected to at least triple, making it easily the greatest natural disaster in United States history.

"You folks have your work cut out for you," he told Lao Ti as he pulled into the parking lot of Oriental Gardens. "The enemy you're up against is a hell of a lot more elusive than most of the scumbags we go up against."

"And just as dangerous," Lao Ti said. "If not more so..."

ORIENTAL GARDENS RESTAURANT was one of Pasadena's prized dining emporiums, located near the Little Switzerland district with its architecturally noteworthy homes. The restaurant had formerly been a private residence designed by the firm of Greene and Greene, and painstaking care had been taken to ensure that the added-on banquet facilities conformed to the discriminating standards of the main house.

Once they were inside, Kissinger and Lao Ti had no trouble tracking down Gadgets Schwarz and Rona Lynne at a table close to the podium where guest speakers would be addressing the gathering later on. For dinner fare, the menu was essentially Chinese, featuring wonton and hot and sour soups, cold spiced salad and entrée choices of tangerine beef, walnut chicken, sweet and sour shrimp or a vegetarian platter.

Once Gadgets and Lao Ti had filled each other in on their recent doings, the conversation drifted back to the subject of earthquakes. When Kissinger mentioned his earlier discussion with Lao Ti about primitive forecasting methods used in the Orient, Rona Lynne was quick to dispel any notion that the Far East was alone in the implementation of such techniques.

"Here in the States we do our share of research into low-tech prediction," she said. "In fact, that's one of the areas we're hoping to make more headway in by collaborating with the OSC."

"Some of our people have been on the cutting edge of the more sophisticated developments, too," Lao Ti said.

"There's an understatement." Rona laughed. "Why, without Shih Consai, it might have been months, maybe even years before we'd have had an open house to show off our laser and particle-beam facilities."

Schwarz asked, "Who's Shih?"

"Practically the patron saint of earthquake prevention," Rona explained. "He came here from China during World War II and got in on the ground floor of the field. He died near here a couple of months ago, but by then he'd almost single-handedly master-minded not only our laser and particle-beam pro-grams, but also the HO-29 quake simulator in Ventura."

"That place where your husband works?" Schwarz asked.

Rona nodded.

Kissinger swallowed a mouthful of chicken and washed it down with his mai tai, then said, "I heard this Shih guy mentioned quite a bit today. Sure sounds like he was quite the genius."

"Without a doubt the most brilliant man I ever worked with," Rona said.

"How'd he die?" Schwarz asked.

Rona told him, "He liked to work at home a lot, so Cal Tech footed the bill to set up a minilab on his property. One night the whole place went up in a horrible explosion. Knocked out windows half a mile away. He was trying to fine-tune a prototype device. There must have been a malfunction."

"I see," Kissinger said. As the conversation went on without him, he found himself distracted by a gnawing flash of déjà vu that had come over him at the mention of the explosion. It didn't take long for him to pinpoint the sensation. Rona's description of the circumstances behind Shih Consai's untimely demise closely paralleled a brush with death Kissinger had had years ago in Wisconsin, where he'd been involved in a brief venture designing a hybrid automatic pistol. His offices had been located above a chemical supply company, and when a flash fire had swept through the downstairs supply room, he'd barely had time to dive two stories to the ground before a blast ripped through the building, supposedly cremating his business partner, Howie Crosley. As it had turned out, Crosley hadn't died in the fire at all, but rather had used it as a cover to leave Wisconsin with plans for the automatic pistol, which he eventually mass-produced in Alabama for sale on the black market. Something about the similarity between the two incidents stuck in Kissinger's mind.

"Excuse me," he said, turning to Rona during a lull in the conversation, "I don't mean to be disrespectful, but I wonder, did they find Shih's body after the explosion?"

Rona hesitated a moment and her voice took on a raspy edge as she nodded and glanced down at the table, whispering, "What was left of it...."

4

When his marriage to Rona went bust, Mel Bronson had instinctively retreated to the past and moved to Ventura, a slowly growing city an hour's drive north of Los Angeles. He'd spent his first fourteen years there, longing for a chance to leave, but now that he'd been back a few months after living twenty-five years in L.A., he found a certain comfort in the nostalgic familiarity of the surroundings. The apartment he'd moved into was just down the block from where he'd grown up, and a lot of the flea markets on Main Street where he'd hung out as a youth were still run by the same men. They all recalled his mechanical prowess and offered him jobs.

Bronson had politely refused the offers, for although he was still intrigued by the challenge of troubleshooting broken appliances taken in by the shops and putting them back in working order, his skills now commanded a higher price. Branching out his expertise into computers, Bronson had ridden the crest of the high-tech revolution, and within two days of returning to Ventura with a glowing résumé, he had secured a job doing computer programming and maintenance at the prestigious California Quakesim Center on Haames Street.

And yet, for all the sophisticated trappings of his present career, there was still a part of Mel Bronson deeply rooted in his blue-collar, working-class upbringing. A good example was his dining habits. Before reporting to Quakesim each night for his graveyard shift, Mel Bronson ritually stopped by Truckers' Heaven, a pit stop just off the Ventura Freeway that provided road jockeys with a place to refuel both their bellies and their eighteen-wheelers. While the trucks filled up on diesel, the drivers would be ensuring their own supply of gas after indulging in any of the greasy-skillet offerings on the menu. Bronson had been a truck mechanic in L.A. years ago, and although he'd long since abandoned the grueling demands of that profession in favor of the cleaner, less physically demanding world of computers, he still enjoyed the atmosphere of truck stops and had a feisty appetite for the likes of the Heavenly B.P. Special, which consisted of well-done minute steak drenched in Worcestershire and barbecue sauce, mounds of catsup-smothered hash browns, green beans shriveled in a special glaze of brown sugar and bacon bits, a slice of deep-dish apple pie and all the scalding java one could handle. The B.P. supposedly stood for Blue Plate, but Bronson and others were certain that bicarbonate and Pepto Bismol were more appropriate derivatives. Oh, but it was so good going down.

Tonight, however, Bronson ate his food without the usual relish, bolting it the way dogs go through a bowlful of kibble. His attention was on a book of computer schematics before him. The top-secret manual was from the Quakesim facility, detailing the inner workings of the multimillion-dollar computer systems that were the backbone of the center's operations. Bronson had clearance to have the manual in his possession because he was one of the four computer experts charged with keeping the equipment in top working order. If anyone happened to see what he was reading, he could easily explain that he was just boning up on his work in hopes of earning a raise.

In truth, though, his reasons for studying the manual were very different.

By the time the waitress had taken away all but his pie and coffee, Bronson felt as well-briefed about the computers as he would ever need to be. As he finished the pie, the balding, mole-faced man turned to the late edition of the *Ventura News*, which carried an in-depth story on the trial of four men and two women who, as part of the radical peace group NOWAR, had successfully bypassed security at a weapons research laboratory in Palo Alto and vandalized expensive equipment before setting fire to the records office on their way out. Antiwar slogans had been spray-painted on the walls and propaganda leaflets had been strewn across the floors—leaflets containing the same NOWAR information sent to the media within hours of the raid.

Bronson carefully scrutinized the reported details of the incident, which had resulted in more than eight million dollars' worth of damage and major setbacks in development of the I-235 series of radarscope homing systems for a new generation of shoulder-mounted nuclear weapons. He was certain that he already knew the modus operandi of NOWAR inside out, but with the moment of execution of his master plan drawing closer, it was important that he had every detail memorized, both in terms of the outfits the peacenik commandos wore and the source material of their handouts.

Fortunately, there were no revelations in the article that would require any drastic changes in the plan. Bronson finished his pie, then had a cigarette with his final refill of coffee. Caffeine was rattling through his system, pricking his nerves to a state of mild agitation and stinging his brain with a heightened sense of awareness. There was plenty of work to be done this evening, and he needed to be as alert as possible to make sure it all came off.

A grease-spattered clock behind the coffee counter read 10:49 when Bronson got up from his booth, leaving a twenty-percent tip before heading to the cashier's station. He exchanged pleasantries with the dowdy woman manning the cash register and bought a pack of Camels. On his way out the door, he peeled off the cellophane and lit up a cigarette, watching as a small, eight-wheel truck pulled into the stop, bearing a decal on its side that read Comp-Tech Supplies.

On the way to his Dodge pickup, Bronson detoured toward the truck, whose driver had just gotten out to pump a load of self-serve gas. The other man was easily a dozen years younger than Bronson, dressed in standard trucker gear of blue jeans and flannel shirt.

"We're all set," the man told Bronson as they passed each other.

"So am I," Bronson said. "All systems go."

Bronson continued walking past the man and climbed into his Dodge. He started the engine and blew smoke at the windshield in a long, sustained exhalation that was part sigh, part release of pent-up anxiety.

This was it. As soon as he pulled out of the truck stop, there would be no turning back.

AS MUCH AS DR. SHIH CONSAI was acclaimed for his input into the development of high-tech means of drilling holes near volatile fault systems, the accomplishment paled alongside his true pride and joy, the HO-29 Quake Simulator. Prior to his untimely death, he had spent the better part of twelve years on the Ventura project—sweating out the operating principles, incorporating supporting data, supervising the construction and seeing to it that the massive undertaking efficiently and effectively performed the task for which it had been created.

When completed five months previously, the HO-29 had looked as if every penny of its $2.5 billion budget had been judiciously spent. In essence, the Quakesim, as it was affectionately known by its caretakers, was an 11,000-square-foot, 234-ton, water-immersed scale model of the California coastline. As accurately as possible, the model recreated the state's geological and seismological makeup, with particular emphasis given to the myriad fault systems that existed along that tender junction between the Pacific and American continental plates. Linked up via a state-of-the-art computer system receiving input from more than three hundred thousand types of monitoring devices located along the San Andreas and other fault lines throughout the state, the HO-29 was rigged to mimic the second-by-second shifting of the actual plates, giving seismologists and geologists an unprecedented opportunity not only to upgrade their understanding of earthquake phenomena, but also to plot a precision-oriented strategy for both predicting and, if possible, preventing the higher-magnitude tremors that posed so great a threat to the state of California.

So sensitive was the Quakesim that it picked up ground vibrations caused by that afternoon's demolition of Wheaton High School in Pasadena and the underground detonation of TNT by an oil firm drilling wells in upper Kern County.

From its Ventura base, the Quakesim system transmitted a backup copy of all computerized findings via satellite to a sister station atop Wisdom Plateau in Eureka Valley near the Nevada border. While the Ventura facility emphasized monitoring, the Wisdom Plateau crew focused on analyzing data, adjusting the countless monitors and, sometime soon, implementing the strategies for trying to prevent earthquakes by the use of nuclear charges to neutralize pressure points along the fault lines.

Mel Bronson was part of the crew responsible for keeping Quakesim healthy and fully operable. With so many billions of computer calculations being made every millisecond throughout the intricate system, it was imperative that glitches be kept to a minimum. Once the HO-29 evolved into its intended use as a mechanical general calling the shots in the war against earthquakes, it wouldn't do to have bogus readings lead to a false alarm evacuating San Francisco during peak rush hours or, even worse, miscalculating the target area for a surgical nuke blast and having a megaquake started instead of prevented.

Bronson pulled up to the security gate of California Quakesim Center at 10:59 p.m. As usual, the complex was relatively quiet, with minimum personnel on hand to gut it out through the graveyard shift. He waved to the guard manning the entrance booth, and when the metal cross-arm swung up in front of his Dodge, Bronson drove onto the lot and eased into a designated parking spot located beneath the yellowish glow of a halogen light mounted atop a nearby pole. As he got out of the pickup, he saw the Comp-Tech truck passing the inspection at the gate and being admitted onto the property.

So far so good.

The employees' entrance was located next to the loading dock. Bronson walked slowly up the steps, noting the truck out of the corner of his eye. It looped around and then backed up to the dock, slowing to a stop against the rubber bumperlike extensions providing protection for both delivery vehicles and the cement framework of the service ramp.

Just as Bronson was reaching for the door, it opened outward and two men in warehouse coveralls emerged in mid-conversation about last night's Lakers game. They halted just in time to avoid colliding with Bronson.

"Ah, Mel, my man." The taller of the workers grinned at Bronson. "Just the dude I been lookin' for. Lakers by twenty-one, in case you missed the sports pages."

"Shit, how 'bout that, Kenny, you lucky slob." Bronson shook his head regretfully and raided his wallet for five dollars, which he passed along to the tall man. "Don't spend it all in one place."

"Got more of these babies to collect, then I'm blowin' 'em all on my sweet li'l poontang!" The worker kissed the bill, then crumpled it into his shirt pocket and went to help his partner unload the Comp-Tech shipment.

Bronson went inside the building and paused in the vacant corridor. There was a peephole through which he was able to look back out at the dock area. Kenny was using a key to open the larger warehouse door while the shorter worker looked over a clipboard in the hands of the driver Bronson had swapped words with at Truckers' Heaven. Off in the background, he could see part of the security gate, but the guard's booth was blocked from view by the Quakesim facility's research and development wing. Conversely, that meant that the guard couldn't see the docks, a factor that played nicely into Bronson's master plan.

When Kenny reappeared on the docks driving a small powerized forklift, the driver unlocked the rear doors of his truck, then quickly jerked them open. Another man inside the truck's hold burst out in a blur of motion, firing a high-powered stun gun at the short warehouse worker. Even as the man was crumpling to the concrete, the driver pulled out a similar weapon and turned it on Kenny, felling the man before he could react.

"Very good," Bronson muttered to himself as he turned and headed down the corridor that eventually took him to an employees' lounge area where, as usual, his three fellow workers were indulging themselves in one last game of poker before going on their shift.

"Hey, Bronson, how's it hangin'?" one of the men called out, looking up through a haze of cigarette smoke.

"Low and long, like always," Bronson said as he grabbed his time card and punched in. "Who cleaned up tonight?"

"I did," the man with the cigarette boasted, raking in the kitty of loose change and dollar bills.

"I swear," Bronson complained good-naturedly, "all the gambling that goes on here, you'd think this was Vegas."

"Shit, this is chump change compared to the shit that goes up at Wisdom Plateau," the winner said. "Those guys boogie across the border on lunch break just so they can wrestle one-armed bandits for five minutes before hustling back."

Bronson's co-workers were rising from their chairs when the door behind them swung open and the Comp-Tech infiltrators charged in, wearing the leaf-green jumpsuits or "uniforms" of the NOWAR commandos. Bronson knew his part and played it to the hilt, trying to head off the men with the stun guns.

"I don't know who you assholes are, but—"

When the tip of a gun was pressed against his forearm, Bronson contorted convincingly and sprawled to the ground. His companions were similarly disabled moments later, then knocked out for a longer duration by quick injections of a sedative. Once the other staff members were disabled, Bronson opened his eyes and rose to his feet.

"Real Oscar performance, there, Mel," one of his co-conspirators told him.

"You, too, Chuck," Bronson said. "For a second there, I thought you were going to pull the trigger on me."

"Be kinda counterproductive to do that, don't you think?"

Bronson nodded as the driver of the Comp-Tech truck handed him a two-way radio and told him, "Picked this off a security guy down the hall."

"Good." Bronson strapped the communicator to his belt. "The guy outside'll call in every couple of hours, so we can keep tabs on him. Now, let's get cracking. We've got a lot of work to do."

For starters, Chuck took a can of spray paint from his belt and handed a second one to the driver. Bronson didn't want to risk having his handwriting recognized, so he refrained from helping the guys spray NOWAR slogans on the walls of the lounge. He went into the hallway, where Chuck had brought along a crateful of sabotage materials on the forklift. Pulling out a handful of Xeroxed fliers declaring NOWAR's belief that the Quakesim project was secretly a cover for Star Wars defense research, Bronson began scattering sheets across the floors and stapling them to the walls. In all, it took only a few minutes to complete the cosmetic portion of their raid.

Once all the paint had been sprayed, the cans were tossed near the unconscious workers and the three men in green proceeded down the hallway to the main chamber, where the huge, monolithic HO-29 Quake Simulator loomed inside its water tank like some strange, bulky sea creature. Along the north wall was the primary complex of computers, a system measuring five feet high and more than forty feet across.

"Okay, we all know our jobs, so get to it." Bronson glanced at an overhead clock, then opened a large kit bag filled with tools and small computer boards. "We've got two hours to pull this off, and every second counts."

CONCURRENTLY WITH the sabotaging of the California Quakesim Center in Ventura, a similar assault was taking place at the Wisdom Plateau facilities in Eureka Valley. Although the remote sprawl of small buildings was fenced-in and subject to round-the-clock patrol by armed guards, these security measures were inadequate when pitted against the determination of Hannas-ma Yang's Yellow River Brigade. As with Mel Bronson in Ventura, the Chinese guerrillas had help on the inside. In this case, it was Art Frank, a dumpy, sallow-faced janitor whose nightly cleaning of the main security office provided him with access to both the central alarm system and the monitor screens linked to remote cameras used for surveillance of the grounds. Frank had been working at Wisdom Plateau for almost two months, during which time he had had ample opportunity to know when the security guards took their breaks and were otherwise in a position of greatest vulnerability. Hannas-ma Yang had already paid him five thousand dollars and was offering another five grand if he succeeded in his chosen mission, thereby matching half his yearly wages, so Frank had taken great pains to prepare for his big moment.

Tonight, as usual, the guard on duty in the main office used the janitor's appearance with an industrial-size vacuum cleaner as an excuse to step out for a cigarette break. Also as usual, Frank had brought the guard a Styrofoam cup filled with fresh coffee from a vending machine located on the far side of the building. Normally, the guard relied on the coffee's caffeine to help keep him awake during his shift. Tonight, however, the powerful sedative Frank had slipped into the drink would undoubtedly lull the man into a catnap within the next five minutes. Frank knew he had the office to himself for at least two minutes. He needed only twenty-five seconds to disconnect the central alarm system and slow down the panning speed of the surveillance camera monitoring the northwest periphery of the grounds.

When the guard returned, exhaling the last puff of his cigarette, he was already stifling a yawn that told Frank the sedative was kicking in. He exchanged a few words with the guard, then went on with his business, fantasizing about the trip to Honolulu he was going to take once he got his second payment from Hannas-ma. Following his benefactor's orders, he shuttled his cleaning supplies to the north building and went to work tidying the administrative and research offices. He was tempted to go and see what it was that the Chinese would be up to once they had access to the restricted west building, but there was no way he was going to jeopardize losing that second five grand. Hannas-ma had told him they merely wanted to gain some information on the earthquake monitoring equipment for use back in their homeland, and that would have to be explanation enough. Besides, as the man had pointed out, the less Frank knew about what he was taking part in, the better.

But curiosity is a powerful force, especially for the weak of will, and a few minutes after going about his business, Art Frank could no longer hold himself back. He knew that in the conference room of the administration building there was a west-facing window that overlooked the smaller complex a hundred yards away. Going into that room and leaving the lights off, the janitor opened the venetian blinds and peered out into the night.

A partial moon spilled enough light across the plateau that he was able to clearly see not only the west building and its twin rooftop satellite dishes, but also the adjacent, empty parking lot and cyclone fence some forty yards beyond. Several minutes passed, then Frank saw four figures appear on the far side of the fence. They set down what looked to be a small trampoline, and in quick succession, three of the men stepped back, took running starts and then leaped onto the trampoline with an artful grace that enabled them to clear the fence with high, somersaulting bounds.

"Whoah!" Frank muttered, awed at the performance like a child watching circus performers in the center ring.

The first two men landed and rolled on impact with the finesse of trained parachutists, coming up uninjured. The third intruder, however, landed awkwardly and remained on the ground, clutching his ankle. He was left behind as the other two proceeded to the west building.

Unlike at the Ventura complex, Wisdom Plateau's computer rooms were not monitored around the clock, and from seven at night until six the following morning the facility was left locked and untended. Frank saw that the Chinese had no trouble getting past the lock and disappeared inside.

Twenty minutes passed, then the intruders emerged from the facilities. The trampoline had since been tossed over the fence and set up so that they could leave the grounds the same way they had entered. The injured man was last to go. He wasn't in a position to try vaulting over the fence, but fortunately it wasn't in the plan for him to do so. Instead, he climbed the fence and used the trampoline as a buffer between himself and the barbed-wire coping. A scrap of canvas from his pants caught on one of the barbs and was torn free as the man lowered himself down the far side.

Seconds later the foursome had slipped off and vanished into the dark of night.

Art Frank, satisfied that he was only a few hours away from his five-grand payoff, confidently strolled down from the conference room and returned to the security office, where he found the guard snoring at his desk. After quickly reactivating the alarm and readjusting the panning speed of the surveillance camera, Frank jostled the guard awake.

"Huh...what?"

"Come on guy, you were snoring so loud, I thought someone was in here with a chain saw," Frank joked. "Thought I'd give you a shake before somebody caught you dozing on the job."

The guard rubbed his eyes and massaged a kink in his neck. "Damn," he groaned, checking his watch. "Thanks, Artie."

"No prob, man."

Frank was just on his way out of the room when there was a sudden explosion that shook the entire building and started the alarm system clanging loudly. The guard was knocked to the floor. Once he staggered to his feet, he and Frank hurried down the corridor to the nearest exit. Rushing out into the night, both men looked toward the west building, which was throwing off twenty-foot-high flames. One of the satellite dishes had toppled to the ground and the other was on its side, looking like a giant witches' cauldron set atop the flames.

Both the guard and Art Frank had the same reaction to the carnage. Slack-jawed, they muttered in unison, "Oh, shit!"

5

"As long as we keep it strictly platonic."

"Fine by me."

"At least for now, that is," Rona Lynne amended. "I'm old-fashioned as far as first dates go."

"Rona, it's no problem," Gadgets Schwarz said as he drove down the sycamore-lined street with his former classmate beside him. "I've had a fun time being with you and I'm not about to spoil things by getting fresh."

"I always knew you were a gentleman."

"Besides," Schwarz said, spotting the headlights closing in behind them, "we're still a foursome, right?"

"Right."

Kissinger and Lao Ti were following them through the Pasadena hills near the Rose Bowl. The dinner conversation at Oriental Gardens had been stimulating enough that the group had decided to follow through on Rona's suggestion that they stop by her place afterward. She promised to raid her wine rack for a bottle of prized '84 Louis Jadot Chardonnay.

Rona's place was a tri-level built on a steep slope at the end of a cloistered cul-de-sac. The driveway was made of small crushed stone and made grinding sounds under the tires of the rental car. As they headed up the walk, Gadgets admired the meticulously groomed lawn and Japanese landscaping. "I never had you pegged as the green thumb type, Rona."

"I'm not," she confessed as she unlocked the door. "My gardener threatens me with shears if I even try to tamper with his handiwork. He's a genius with plants."

Inside, the house was sparsely but tastefully furnished, combining high tech and Oriental touches. "I owe a lot of my tastes to Dr. Shih," Rona explained. "His place was in *Architectural Digest* and *House and Garden*. If I ever saw something I liked over there, he'd always tell me where in town to get the best deal on something along the same line. He's the one that turned me on to my gardener, too."

"Generous guy," Schwarz said. "Too bad about what happened to him."

"It sure is." Rona noticed that the red light on her answering machine was blinking. As Kissinger and Lao Ti came in to join the party, she checked the tape and heard a brief message from one of her co-workers at Cal Tech, who had phoned only a few minutes before and wanted Rona to call back as soon as she got in, no matter how late.

"Sounds serious," Schwarz said.

"Hard to tell with Julie, but I'd better make sure," Rona said. "Look, make yourselves at home. The wine's over there in the rack. A fire would be nice, too."

Rona excused herself and headed up a short flight of carpeted steps to the master bedroom. Gadgets tracked down the Chardonnay and attacked the bottle with a corkscrew, while Kissinger went to the fireplace and opened the damper before lighting a match to the kindling beneath a pile of pine logs stacked in the hearth. Almost immediately the flames took to the dry wood and began throwing off heat into the large living room.

Lao Ti stood before a picture window offering a view of the deep valley that sheltered the Rose Bowl. Vacant in the moonlight, the stadium looked massive, almost surreal, like a parked spaceship. "Football season's one of the things I missed most back in Taipei," Lao reflected. "Maybe if I'm still here by New Year's I'll come out for the bowl game."

"Why wait that long?" Kissinger said. "The Rams are in town next weekend. Unless something comes up and we get called back to Virginia, I can get tickets and we could make a day of it."

"That'd be great," Lao said.

"What about us?" Gadgets asked the woman. "Don't you miss us, just a little?"

"That goes without saying and you know it," Lao Ti said. "Hardly a day goes by that I don't think about you guys and some of the things we went through."

Schwarz passed out the wine and for a few minutes the three of them shared a few reminiscences of their exploits over the years, the kind of life-and-death moments that create a special bond between those who survive them. As with strong family ties, the threesome were at ease and comfortable together, carrying on as if Lao Ti hadn't been gone for almost a year. A toast was proclaimed by Schwarz, and the three of them sipped in tribute to "the Farm."

"Any chance you'd want to come back to Stony Man?" Kissinger asked at one point. "We never really replaced you, you know."

Lao Ti smiled. "I'm flattered. But I like what I'm doing now. It's a whole different environment, and sometimes I miss the action a lot, but there's still a lot of payoffs."

"I imagine it's always exciting to be at the forefront of a new frontier," Kissinger said.

"Yes, it is," Lao admitted. "Not that I didn't enjoy the time I spent at the Farm . . . excluding the last part, of course."

Rona returned from upstairs, her face taut with worry. Schwarz could see the anxiety in her eyes.

"Rona, what's wrong?"

Rona took her wine and sipped it, not so much to savor the taste as to wet the dryness that had crept into her throat.

"Some peace group broke into the Quakesim Center," she reported. "They knocked out my husband and the other workers, then vandalized the whole main building."

"Oh, no . . ." Lao Ti gasped.

"How bad?" Kissinger asked.

"We aren't sure yet," she explained. "The Quakesim's still working, but the monitoring signals have been all fouled up. They can't get any in-house readings, and they aren't sure yet where the satellite data's being sent to."

"It goes to Wisdom Plateau, doesn't it?" Lao Ti asked.

"Normally, yes," Rona said. "But there was a raid there, too. The receiving station's been knocked out."

RONA LYNNE WAS MISTAKEN about Dr. Shih Consai in more ways than one.

Even as she had been speaking in the past tense about his influence on her and his great love of the finer things in life, the supposedly long-dead Chinese scientist was sitting in an enclosed patio area behind a run-down fish hatchery near Big Pine, a small Owens Valley town best known for its view of the Rocky Mountains.

The sixty-five-year-old man, wearing a white laboratory jacket and puffing on a long, thin-stemmed ivory pipe, sat in a weathered rattan rocker, staring out at the distant mountains and the sprinkling of stars behind them.

"Do you read the stars, Dr. Yurvi?" he asked his companion, the Romanian physicist who had disappeared from Cumberland Nuclear Research Center in the wake of the recent plutonium theft. Yurvi was a few years younger than Shih, though there were more signs of age on his pale face. He stopped pacing and glanced down at the other man.

"No, and I don't read fortune cookies, either," he snapped irritably, "so spare me any more of your 'Confucius says' drivel!"

Shih took his pipe from his lips and smiled menacingly. "Your prejudice is showing, Dr. Yurvi. You shouldn't let your impatience get the better of you so easily."

"*That's* what I'm talking about!" Yurvi shouted. "You're always talking down to everyone here like

you're some philosophy teacher trying to enlighten his students. I'm fed up with it, do you understand?''

Shih rose from the rocker and walked to the edge of the patio. He turned and glanced back at Yurvi, clucking his tongue. ''The Great Wall is nothing compared to the chip on your shoulder, Dr. Yurvi. Since you despise me so much, you will excuse me if I leave you to your misery.''

''You can dive into one of the fish tanks and drown for all I care,'' the Romanian told him.

''I already died once.'' Shih chuckled. ''I am in no hurry to use up yet another of my lives.''

Actually, Shih's death had been largely vicarious, carried out in the person of a slain illegal alien Hannas-ma Yang had placed behind Shih's Pasadena home the night the scientist's laboratory had exploded. Neither Shih nor his classified prototype for the laser drilling system had been anywhere near the area at the time of the ''accident'' that had supposedly taken his life. Both the scientist and his latest creation had already come north to the fish hatchery inherited by Hannas-ma Yang after the death of his great-uncle five years earlier.

While fish were still bred in large tanks and deep holding bays on the property's six acres, the operation was now essentially a front behind which Hannas-ma's California branch of the Yellow River Brigade based itself. Inconspicuous enough on the outside, the main building housed equipment and supplies that had nothing to do with helping to replenish fishing waters in the Owens Valley. A discerning eye might have suspected as much at the sight of three sentries armed with M-14s who patrolled the

grounds, which had been deliberately overgrown with oleander and other high-growing bushes to add to the hatchery's already isolated position four miles off the main highway.

Leaving the patio, Shih tapped out his pipe and glanced up at the roof overhead. Montgomery Landlicott, the security guard who had helped Yurvi take flight from Cumberland with their stolen supply of plutonium, was positioned in a makeshift sniper's nest, sitting with his feet propped up while he tinkered with the Stoner 63 rifle he'd brought with him from West Virginia. The Stoner, built by the creator of the legendary M-16, was a weapon composed of interchangeable parts that could allow for its quick transformation into six different setups, ranging from an assault rifle to a fixed tank machine gun.

"You oughta go easy on the doc," Landlicott advised Shih, having obviously heard the exchange on the patio. "Poor guy got put to work nonstop while he was still jet-lagged. Who wouldn't wig out a little going seventy-two hours straight?"

"I'll keep that in mind, soldier," Shih called up to the sniper. "And perhaps you should keep in mind that you're on lookout up there."

"Hey, I don't tell you how to do your job, doc," Landlicott sneered. He slammed a magazine into his Stoner. "Not to worry. Anyone comes creeping this way that ain't supposed to, they get a hot shower, know what I mean?"

"I'm feeling more secure already," Shih said, making no effort to conceal his sarcasm.

Not yet ready to forsake the fresh night air, the Chinese scientist wandered out to the large holding

tanks, which reflected the moonlit sky overhead. Occasionally a trout would disrupt the mirrorlike surface in pursuit of a fly or water strider, making gentle lapping sounds. Shih was reminded of his *koi* fish pond back in Pasadena, and he felt a moment's nostalgia for the life he had left behind. Had he really made the right decision when he agreed to throw in his valued expertise with a renegade like Hannas-ma Yang and his Yellow River Brigade? All that early talk about helping his native China to regain a spot at the center of the world stage had certainly been intoxicating, as had been the prospect of spearheading his homeland's technological passage into the twenty-first century as the highest-ranking scientist in all of China. But could the Yellow River Brigade seriously be expected to carry out such grandiose plans, especially when their implementation required an alliance with the Soviets?

He'd gone back and forth on the issue countless times since making his decision, and in the end he always reached the same conclusion. What was done was done. He'd made his choice and there could be no turning back. If he were to renounce the Brigade and go back to his American colleagues, he had no doubt but that he would face prison, perhaps even death as a traitor, given the passage of recent legislation regarding terrorist-related activity. In any event, they would never allow him to engage in his livelihood or to enjoy the kind of life he'd had up to the night his laboratory had gone up in smoke.

"Iacta alea est," he whispered to himself. The die is cast. His only choice was to commit himself totally to the course he'd set and hope that through his ef-

forts the seemingly impossible dream might become a reality.

Before returning to the main building, Shih looked past the tanks to a stand of cottonwoods just inside the northern periphery of the hatchery grounds. The guerrilla who had died in the Winnebago en route to Big Pine had been buried in a shallow grave between two of the taller trees, and Shih saw that one of the sentries was now standing near the spot, looking down at the disturbed ground. Although he was more than twenty yards away from the soldier, Shih could hear the man's suppressed weeping, and out of respect the scientist turned and went back to the main building. Landlicott had assumed a more vigilant position atop the roof, and he deliberately looked away from Shih as the older man passed by.

Once inside, the first room Shih came to was brightly lit and warm, both from lights and from the equipment in use there. With its workbenches, cubicles, chalkboards, computers and laboratory furnishings, this was the domain he shared with his unlikely associate, Dr. Yurvi. Despite their mutual antagonism and differing reasons for being in Big Pine, the two men were bound by a common cause, having been brought together largely through the efforts of Hannas-ma Yang. The collaborative fruit of their labors was visible in the middle of the room, where Shih was modifying his prototype laser drill in such a way that it could be used to bore deep holes in the earth of a diameter suitable for delivery of the XT-22 nuclear warheads Yurvi was arming and adapting for their newly intended application. As Shih looked over the project and the adjacent chalkboard with its scrawled

formulas and diagrams that were indecipherable by anyone but the two scientists, he was able to put aside his antipathy for Yurvi and focus on the more important matter of ensuring the success of their endeavor.

Everything was in readiness save for two factors. One was in the hands of Hannas-ma Yang and his contacts in Ventura, so Shih only concerned himself with the second matter, that of correctly calibrating the tension requirements for braces that would hold the laser in steady alignment with its coordinates as it released its concentrated ray of energy down into the earth. Properly stabilized, the laser would successfully penetrate the earth to required depths more than forty times faster than any other means, and with less disruption of adjacent land masses. But if the weapon was too loosely mounted, vibration could cause the whole apparatus to jolt on its moorings, thereby risking that an errant blast would only mildly scar the earth. And if there wasn't some measure of give when the laser was triggered, the weapon's massive bulk would be capable of snapping those same mounts and causing the weapon to malfunction, or worse. The explosion that had rocked Shih Consai's laboratory five months earlier had deliberately mimicked the destructive power of the transmitter in a state of uncontrolled overload.

As Shih worked at the chalkboard, periodically using the eraser and chalk to make changes in the calculations, he heard the door behind him open. Dr. Yurvi entered and slowly came beside him. Neither man looked at the other, but rather concentrated on the white scrawls before them. It took Yurvi a few minutes to take note of the changes Shih had made and comprehend a new line of thinking, but once he was attuned to the older man's reasoning, he suddenly gasped with excitement and grabbed for a piece of chalk.

"May I?" he asked Shih, showing no signs of his earlier anger.

"Please," Shih said with a wave of his hand.

Yurvi attacked the board like a man possessed, raising a small cloud of chalk dust with the eraser and making staccato sounds with the rapid play of his chalk across the green slate. When he was finished, he took a step back and beamed at his work. "There!"

Shih Consai rubbed his thumb along the underside of his chin as he took in the new data. A smile crept slowly across his face, this one far less adversarial than the one he'd worn out on the patio. "Very good, Dr. Yurvi," he murmured, genuinely impressed. "We should double-check everything on the computers, but I think you've solved it."

"I just built on what you started, Shih," Yurvi conceded. There was a conciliatory tone in his voice. "I'm sorry for blowing up at you out there on the patio."

"Better you than this, yes?" Shih said, gesturing at the workbench where one of the retooled warheads rested on foam cushions.

"Very much so." Yurvi laughed, wearing away at the last of the tension that had been building between the two men over the past three days.

Side by side, they went into an adjacent room, roughly the same size as the laboratory, which was filled on one side with computer equipment and on the other with a gridwork of radar scanning screens, ra-

The men downed the small portions of wine, then went back to their tasks. Several minutes later, they heard the rumbling of a Jeep headed toward the hatchery. The vehicle slowed to a stop alongside the main building, parking behind the Winnebago.

Hannas-ma Yang led his brother and the other two night raiders into the laboratory. The man with the injured ankle immediately retreated to a cot in the far corner, where he began to massage the swollen extremity.

"How did it go?" Yurvi asked, stepping out of the computer room.

"As planned," Hannas-ma gloated. "And you?"

"We've made a breakthrough on the brace mounts," Yurvi divulged, "and Shih says that we are now receiving data from the HO-29 in Ventura."

"We are and they aren't," the terrorist leader said. "Excellent. Then all is readiness. Dr. Shih, when do you think we will be able to proceed to the next step?"

Shih poked his head out of the computer room and told the others, "Tomorrow."

6

Hal Brognola drove with FBI agent Stan Turdrin to Frostburg, a small town located just west of Cumberland along Route 40. The two men were roughly the same age, though Turdrin had more boyish features despite the fact his hair had turned prematurely white.

"Even up here we've heard a few tales about Able Team," Turdrin said as he guided his Toyota Celica down the winding ribbon of asphalt. "Frankly, I figured you'd be the one with the gray hairs after having to deal with such a rowdy crew."

"Oh, they're not much trouble," Brognola said, chewing on a cigar as he admired the scenery. "As long as I keep them off the leash as much as possible they'll respond within expectations. Or beyond expectations, I should say."

"Isn't it a little unnerving to be responsible for an outfit that routinely bends rules to the breaking point, though?"

Brognola shrugged. "If I didn't expect it of them, maybe it'd be a problem. But, after all, Stan, that's our mission. The grayer the area, the more apt they are to make the best of things." The Stony Man head of operations offered the FBI agent a sly smile. "Maybe you're a little jealous, hmm?"

"No question," Turdrin said. "If the Bureau spent less time playing 'Mother, May I' with regulatory boards and more time going up against the vermin, we'd nip a lot of these problem groups in the bud before they had a chance to pull off the kind of stunts we're up against now."

"Yeah, there's a lot to be said for a nice low-level preemptive strike," Brognola mused. "But unfortunately it's too late for that with this case. We're just going to have to figure out a way to squeeze these bastards back into the tube."

When they reached the turnoff for a small county airfield, Turdrin pulled into the parking lot and found a space near the control tower. The two men got out and walked past the rows of small Cessnas and Beechcrafts lined across the tarmac.

"We're working on the assumption that Yurvi and Landlicott are somehow tied into the whole mess on the West Coast," Turdrin explained. "We've checked through all the flight manifests hoping to turn up any destination points near Ventura or Wisdom Plateau, or up in Oregon."

"Most of these puddle jumpers aren't up to that long a haul," Brognola ventured. "Odds are they just took a short hop somewhere, then switched over to bigger transport."

"We're covering that angle, too," Turdrin said, holding open the side door to the control tower. There was a small ground-floor office, where another FBI agent was talking with a worried-looking man in his early sixties.

"Got our guy," Turdrin's associate announced, gesturing to the older man. "Name's Gil Hovenor."

"Oh, yeah?" Turdrin turned to Hovenor, whose overweight frame strained at the polyester of his jogging suit. His pudgy fingers were covered with rings, and a gold chain dangled from his neck. Although it was cool in the room, sweat beaded on his forehead.

"Like I told him," Hovenor pleaded, indicating the other agent, "I didn't know nothing about any illegal shit."

"Tell me about it," Turdrin said, pulling up a chair. Brognola sat next to him.

"Shit, I just went through the whole thing once," Hovenor complained.

"That was dress rehearsal," Turdrin said. "This is show time. If you're telling the truth, it shouldn't be any problem."

Hovenor went through his pockets for a pack of cigarettes and nervously lit one before beginning. He pointed to photos of Yurvi and Landlicott on the table in front of him. "These guys came by last week, said they were both getting married next weekend and they wanted to fly out to Vegas for a last fling before puttin' on the chains. They wanted to go in style and offered five grand to rent my old DC-3. It's a beaut. I can show it to you—"

"Later," Turdrin said. "Go on."

"Well, it was a nice offer and I hadn't been to Vegas for a while, so, what the hell, I took 'em up on it and flew 'em out there myself."

"Just the two of them in a plane that size?"

Hovenor nodded. "They brought a couple big steamer trunks with 'em, though. Didn't tell me what was in them and I didn't figure it was my business to ask. Your friend won't tell me, but I guess they were smuggling something, right?"

"It still isn't your business to ask, Mr. Hovenor," Turdrin told him. "So, you took them to Vegas. Then what?"

"That's it. I dropped them off, and they had some friends in a Winnebago there waitin' for 'em. They gave me my money plus a five hundred dollar tip and went off in the motor home."

"Didn't you expect to bring them back?" Brognola questioned.

Hovenor nodded. "Yeah, but they said they didn't want to be tied down to a specific departure time. I know how that goes in Vegas. Sometime your luck's bad and you can't wait to leave, but other times—"

"That's okay, Mr. Hovenor," Turdrin said. "Did you get a look at the people who picked them up? Maybe a license number of the Winnebago?"

Hovenor shook his head. "Hey, I'm a retired contractor, not some private eye. Come to think of it, though, I seem to remember the 'bago's driver being Japanese, maybe Chinese. But that's about it."

Turdrin had been jotting notes throughout the whole proceedings. He made a last few scribbles on his pad, looked the whole mess over, then glanced back at Hovenor. "I guess that will be all for now."

"I can go, then?"

Turdrin nodded. "Just don't go too far. We'll check out your story and then get back to you. If you think of anything else, give us a call at this number." He handed Hovenor a slip of paper.

"I'm not . . . you're not going to arrest me?"

"Not unless we find reason to, Mr. Hovenor. Have a nice day."

Hovenor mumbled a few words of thanks to the men who had detained him, then left the tower and crossed the airstrip to his DC-3, barely visible inside one of the far hangars.

"Well, we know how they got out there," Turdrin mused to his confederates once they were alone. "And Wisdom Plateau is only an hour's drive from Vegas. There's got to be some kind of connection."

"But that place is just a monitoring station for earthquake studies, isn't it?" Brognola asked.

Turdrin replied, "Yeah, and so is the place in Ventura that got hit by that NOWAR group. I don't get it."

"Me either," Brognola said.

"Whatever's going on, we better get a handle on it quick," the FBI man declared. "Because if Yurvi gets even one bomb out of that plutonium, there's going to be some serious problems."

TURDRIN AND BROGNOLA returned to the Cumberland Nuclear Research Center just in time to brief heads of the growing ad hoc force that was being assembled to deal with the crisis surrounding the missing plutonium. The meeting room where Able Team had first conferred with Joseph Corriter was now filled with prestigious figures, and sandwiches had been brought in so that the people could keep up on the latest developments without breaking from the task at hand.

Chairing the informal meeting was Milton Green, the Department of Energy's ranking field agent in

Cumberland. He was a frail, anemic-looking man with a propensity for bow ties and sweater vests. His co-workers called him Greendenbacher, no doubt alluding to his vague resemblance to popcorn peddler Orville Redenbacher. Corriter and Carl Lyons were there, as were Pol Blancanales and representatives from three other agencies that had been alerted to the problem—William Shake from the Office of Emergency Preparedness, Tiffany Motain of the National Security Agency, and Brigadier General Edward Vaughn of the Joint Chiefs of Staff.

"After a thorough check of inventories at all other nuclear plants under our jurisdiction," Green told the group, "it seems clear there's been no significant loss of either bomb-grade uranium or plutonium beyond that lost here at Cumberland. That's reassuring only in the sense that we can narrow our investigation. It doesn't change the fact that this Landlicott fellow and Dr. Yurvi have enough plutonium to arm as many as five XT-22s."

"And since they apparently flew to Vegas with their payload," Lyons said, "it seems reasonable to assume they're rendezvousing somewhere in that vicinity with the people behind the warhead heist in Oregon."

Brognola finished a bite of his sandwich, then asked the group, "I wonder if there's some sort of connection between this situation and those NOWAR raids in California, especially that one at Wisdom Plateau."

"I've been thinking some about that, and somehow it just doesn't fit," Turdrin ventured. "The Bureau has a thick file on NOWAR, and it's clear that while they have no qualms about destroying property, murder's not their modus operandi. I don't see them being party to that massacre in Oregon, and they sure as hell wouldn't be stealing plutonium to make bombs. If they were backing Yurvi, they would have already called a press conference to brag about the theft.''

"As a matter of fact," Bill Shake reported, "NO-WAR did call a press conference this morning, but they categorically denied any involvement in what's going on."

"But what about all those spray-painted slogans and pamphlets left behind in Ventura?" Blancanales asked.

"A smoke screen, obviously," General Vaughn belted out in the commanding voice that had served him so well earlier in his career as a drill sergeant. He was a stocky, barrel-chested man with ruddy features and short-cropped hair. "Somebody wanted the world to think NOWAR was behind it, and I'll bet my friggin' stars it's those bastards that killed my men in the Harney Basin!"

"If that's the case, it still brings us back to my question," Brognola said. "What's the connection? Who would get themselves armed with nuclear warheads and then do all this sabotage stuff with the earthquake facilities?"

"Maybe we need a better idea of exactly what was compromised by that sabotage," Turdrin speculated. "According to the briefs I received about the pamphlets left in Ventura, NOWAR supposedly was knocking out the places because they had some sort of vague military application."

"Oh, balls!" Vaughn scoffed. "What'd they think, the Pentagon wants to learn how to predict earthquakes in Russia so we can send armies to go jump up and down on their fault lines to make 'em cause more damage?''

The general was being facetious, but half the people in the room almost simultaneously looked at the man as if he'd just unlocked the key to the puzzle. William Shake from the OEP put the revelation into words. "Of course," he muttered. "Of course! That's it!''

"What?" Corriter said. "Come on, the guy was kidding.''

Tiffany Motain, a stoic woman in her early fifties turned to the security officer sitting beside her and explained. "He might have been kidding, but he's on the right track. Instead of sending armies to go jump on Russia's fault lines, it could very well be that these people plan to use the warheads to trigger quakes in California.''

"Whoa," Lyons said, shaking his head. "That sounds a little farfetched to me.''

"I'm afraid it isn't," Bill Shake said. "Our California office has been working with people at Cal Tech, and there's been a lot of progress made in the area of quake prevention, particularly involving the use of nuclear charges to neutralize seismologically sensitive areas. In fact, one of the long-term functions of the Quake Simulator in Ventura was to serve as an aid in pinpointing locations for quake-control measures.''

"The same simulator that was sabotaged?" Corriter asked.

After Shake nodded, FBI agent Turdrin said, "Okay, if we can assume that we have terrorists out in

California who are putting together the means of starting a major earthquake, we also have to assume that they aren't just bluffing, because there's been no communication from them. No political demands, no ideological rantings. Nothing. People, we have to act on the premise that these people aren't interested in negotiating. My guess is they're just going to go ahead and strike."

"But why?" Tiffany wondered aloud. Worry was obvious in her features. "We're talking about major destruction here. Thousands, maybe hundreds of thousands of lives. They have to have some kind of reason for what they're doing."

"They're psycho, that's why," Corriter ventured.

"Whatever the case," Bill Shake continued, "as head of the Office of Emergency Preparedness, I can tell you all that if the public catches wind of what's at stake here, we're going to have a panic like we've never seen before. This whole operation has to proceed with the highest confidentiality. I can't stress that enough."

"Seems to me it's a little late for that," Lyons said. "I mean, the press had been reporting what they know about all of this, and once they start making the same connections we have, it's going to be on the front pages and at the top of the eleven o'clock news on every station from Bangor to Barstow."

"Man, and when that happens," Joe Corriter predicted, "the shit is really going to hit the fan."

7

As their chartered jet whisked across the parched desert of Eureka Valley and began circling for a landing, Gadgets Schwarz and John Kissinger got their first glimpse of the Wisdom Plateau Monitoring Station. A thin black tendril of smoke rose from the charred shell that had once been the computerized alter ego of Ventura's HO-29 Quake Simulator. Fire crews were still hosing down wreckage, while off near the perimeter fence investigators could be seen scanning the terrain for clues as to the identity of those who had raided the facility the night before.

"Really did a number on that station," Schwarz commented.

Kissinger nodded. "Plastic explosives, I'll bet. Whoever's behind it, they sure as hell knew what they were doing. No way are they going to be able to salvage anything in that mess."

Schwarz and Kissinger had boarded the plane two hours before, shortly after receiving a call from Hal Brognola in Cumberland. All of Stony Man's domestic personnel were now officially plugged into the emergency task force assigned to deal with the spate of guerrilla activities that had hit the West Coast over the past thirty-six hours. At the same time Schwarz and

Kissinger were about to touch down at Wisdom Plateau, Lyons, Blancanales and Brognola were preparing to board a military transport plane that Jack Grimaldi would pilot to Los Angeles, where the troubleshooting force was setting up its California base of operations. And, after briefing backup workers at the Farm, Aaron Kurtzman would be taking a separate flight to Ventura, where he planned to lend his computer expertise in the effort to undo the sabotage to the main computers at the Quakesim facility. Lao Ti and Rona Lynne were already on their way to Ventura for the same reason.

"Rona seems like a real nice lady, Gadgets," Kissinger said as the men braced themselves for landing. "Did I detect a little spark between you guys?"

"The woman's still married," Schwarz said, yawning to unclog his ears from the altitude change.

"That doesn't answer my question," Kissinger said.

"It's just a friendship," Schwarz insisted. "I don't see it going any further than that for the time being."

"I'm impressed with her," Kissinger went on. "You know, we've been meaning to fill Lao Ti's spot at the Farm for some time now, and—"

"Let's not jump the gun, Cowboy," Schwarz told him. "For starters, I doubt that she'd be interested. This gig at Cal Tech seems to agree with her, and she's been a Californian all her life, so I don't think that uprooting to Virginia would appeal to her."

"It was just a thought," Kissinger said.

The jet, a twelve-seat Aerowyld CS-9, dropped smoothly toward the runway adjacent to the Wisdom Plateau complex. Within a split second after making contact with the tarmac, both men could feel the jet's spoilers come into play, neutralizing the craft's lift and beginning the engine-growling process of slowdown. Besides the pilot and co-pilot, there were four other men on the plane, all members of the Ventura Quakesim team. During the entire flight they had been huddled together, discussing strategies for the best way to set up a makeshift receiving system to handle at least some of the functions that had been compromised by the explosion of the main station. Once the jet came to a stop and the passengers were allowed to disembark, the foursome quickly made its way across the runway to where the replacement monitoring equipment, which had been shipped from Colorado manufacturers responding to last-minute orders from the quake-control administration offices in Los Angeles, was being unloaded from two cargo planes.

"Those guys have their work cut out for them," Kissinger said as he and Schwarz headed in the opposite direction, toward the team of investigators casing out the section of fence over which the saboteurs had apparently gained access to the grounds. In charge of the group was a lean, red-haired woman in a conservative gray pantsuit. When she turned to face the visitors, a flash of recognition came to her eyes.

"Why, Mr. Schwarz," she said, offering her hand. "Long time no see."

"Ms Farrell," Schwarz said, shaking her hand. "Good to see a familiar face here."

The two of them were familiar from Able Team's recent assignment in San Diego, when they'd thwarted old nemesis Le Van Than's collaboration with the KGB in attempts to breach security at the Navy's installations in the California border city. Monica Farrell had been the FBI's field officer assigned to the case, and although she'd had only brief contact with the men from Stony Man Farm, an impression had obviously been made.

"Ms Farrell, this is John Kissinger," Schwarz said, handling introductions. "He's our ace weaponsmith, but now and then he likes to get out of the lab and get his hands dirty with the rest of us."

"They're clean at the moment, though," Kissinger said with a grin, extending his hand to shake Farrell's. The two made eye contact and, watching, Schwarz had to suppress a grin of his own. He'd seen that kind of look exchanged before, and knew the inevitable consequences.

"So," Schwarz said, glancing past Farrell at the man around the fence. "Making any headway here?"

"Actually, yes," Farrell said, unlocking her gaze from Kissinger's and getting back to the business at hand. "Things are falling into place rather nicely so far."

"Oh, yeah?" Schwarz said. "When we got the call to head up here, it sounded like everything was coming up zero."

"What a difference a couple hours can make," Farrell said. "Let me bring you up-to-date.

"For starters, on a long shot we put out an APB for a Winnebago with an Oriental driver...which is about all we had on the people who picked up Landlicott and Yurvi in Vegas over the weekend. Needle in a haystack, right?"

"Yeah, to put it mildly," Kissinger said.

"Well, we got the Highway Patrol in on it, and an officer doing border checks struck pay dirt over in

Oasis, just a few miles from here. Seems there was a Winnebago that made a food-and-fuel stop there last night, about three hours before the raid. Driver was Chinese. The guy who runs the station says at least three other men were with him. Two of them turned up on the security cameras when they paid for gas and sandwiches.

"We blew up a still frame to get mug shots and ran a check through our files. Bingo, both of them are listed as being part of the Yellow River Brigade."

"Haven't heard of them," Schwarz said. "New outfit?"

"Pretty new," Farrell explained. "They're a real fringe group. Want to oust the powers that be in both Russia and China and replace them with people who'll forge a unified alliance."

"What a pipe dream," Kissinger reflected. "There'll be a Jewish Pope before that happens."

"Well, obviously they don't believe that," Farrell said. Diverting her gaze to the ruined reception station, she added, "And it looks like they're going to some pretty radical extremes to get their way."

"Then you're certain they're behind this?" Schwarz asked.

The woman nodded. "There's the guy who confirmed it."

She pointed in the direction of the administration building, where two county sheriff's officers could be seen leading Art Frank to their waiting patrol car. The maintenance man had his hands cuffed behind his back and he walked with his head turned down, his face etched with the look of a man who has realized, far too late, that he's gotten into something way over his head.

"Who's he?" Schwarz said.

The FBI agent divulged his identity and the bogus cover story Frank had swallowed when agreeing to assist the Brigade in its plan to infiltrate the Wisdom Plateau complex.

"What a jerk," Kissinger muttered as he watched Frank being driven away. "It's amazing how little it takes to get some people to sell out these days. I mean, he had to know there was more going on than what they told him, but he sees some big bucks and wears them like blinders."

"Well, he's not stupid, that's for sure," Farrell said. "We couldn't get word one out of him until he brought in a lawyer, and then we had to cut a deal that'll get him off with a wrist slap for his part in the whole thing."

Although every member of the Able Team and Stony Man Farm was highly intelligent, Gadgets Schwarz was far and away the most analytical thinker of the group, and all the while he was digesting Monica Farrell's revelations, he was applying the data to the scraps of information that had so far come to his attention in the unwinding crisis. "Okay," he said, thinking aloud, "let's see where we stand now.

"Since we've got this Yellow River Brigade linked to Yurvi and Landlicott by virtue of the Winnebago, it's safe to assume they had something to do with the train raid in Oregon, right?"

"That's the premise we're working on," Farrell agreed.

Schwarz went on, "And since they went to all the trouble to knock out this receiving station, they obviously also had something to do with what happened to the Quakesim in Ventura."

"Right again." Farrell went along with Schwarz's train of thought. "And because, near as we can figure, the Quakesim is still beaming out its reading somewhere that we haven't been able to track, it's a good guess that the Brigade has somehow arranged to monitor those signals."

"Yeah," Schwarz said. "That seems to be what's going on. The word we got before we headed up here was that we're dealing with people who had the means of starting a major quake. It's nice that we know who we're up against, but now we have to figure out where the hell they're operating from."

"We hope to make some headway on that front, soon," Farrell said. Pointing out her associates near the fence, she told Kissinger and Schwarz, "We've got plaster casts of footprints and tire tracks, along with a scrap of clothing one of them lost getting over the fence. The lab's working everything top priority, so with any luck they might turn up something soon."

"What do we do in the meantime?" Kissinger wondered.

"We wait, unfortunately," Farrell said. "Once they've got the fire out, we'll go through the rubble and see if there are any clues there, but other than that—"

A beeper on the agent's belt came to life. She turned it off and excused herself. As the two men watched her head for a nearby sedan, Gadgets turned to Kissinger.

"You're drooling, Cowboy."

Kissinger shrugged his shoulders. "I don't know what you're talking about."

"Uh-huh, right," Schwarz said.

"Okay, so she's attractive," Kissinger conceded. "I've got other things on my mind right now."

"Hey," Schwarz teased, "you were so eager to play cupid with me and Rona. What gives, you can't take what you dish out?"

The two men were still giving each other a hard time when agent Farrell got back out of the car and hurried toward them in long strides. There was a look of excitement on her face that could mean only one thing.

"Found them?"

"Maybe so," Farrell said. "They did an analysis on the piece of clothing. Turned up a strong fish smell. Well, guess what? We got a rap-and-info sheet on one of those guys we identified on the Oasis tape. Guy named Jon Yang. Did a short stint on grand theft auto five years ago. His probation sheet listed his guardian as an uncle who owned a fish hatchery near Big Pine."

"Past tense?" Schwarz said.

"Right," Farrell said. "Uncle's dead. Hatchery's now in Jon's brother's name. Hannas-ma Yang. Mr. Yellow Brigade himself."

8

It was, all in all, the most tranquil time of year in Mammoth Lakes. The summer throng of hikers had dwindled appreciably, and it would be weeks before the first snowfall of the season whitened Mammoth Mountain, so the inevitable crunch of ski-hungry maniacs had yet to descend upon the resort town, located an hour's drive north of Big Pine. By and large, the five hundred year-round residents had their elevated slice of rugged Eden to themselves, and the pace of the town was slow and easy. When a weather-beaten Winnebago rolled down the main road, no one paid it a second glance, save for an early-morning jogger, who nodded a greeting to Hannas-ma Yang, who returned the gesture with an innocent smile as he drove past.

Beyond the heart of town lay two hundred thousand acres comprising Mammoth Lakes Recreation Area. Adorning the rolling hills and mountain ranges were sprawling forests of majestic lodgepole and Jeffrey pines, tall sentries overlooking alpine lakes and the extensive honeycomb of dirt hiking paths that wound through the lush wilderness. Nature lovers could choose from a number of eye-boggling excursions, from the Pacific Crest Trail, Devil's Postpile

National Monument, Rainbow Falls or the John Muir
Trail. Although one was always apt to run into another hiker close to the main trailheads, the more determined souls could set out on their own and within
an hour find themselves pleasurably alone and free to
commune with the elements without human contact.
It was to just such an isolated area that Hannas-ma
Yang was heading.

Using data gleaned from their interception of the
HO-29 Quake Simulator's satellite signals, the Yellow River Brigade was bound for a remote section of
wilderness where the United States Geological Survey
had several monitoring sites. To reach their intended
destination, it was necessary for Hannas-ma Yang to
stray from the main access road and coax the Winnebago along the steep incline of the firebreak. Given the
incredible weight the vehicle was carrying, the drive
was no easy feat, and the altitude's detrimental effect
on the vehicle's carburetor further complicated their
progress. A few hundred yards up the long slope
Hannas-ma was finally forced to stop.

"Everyone out," he told the others. "Jon, set up
the blockade. The others can meet me at the site."

Shih Consai, Jon Yang and three fellow brigadiers
quickly exited the vehicle, taking with them several
bright orange traffic cones and a sign that read: Restricted Area—Keep Out. Dr. Yurvi was more reluc-
tant to follow Hannas-ma's command.

"I am not a young man," Yurvi complained, staring through the windshield at the long hike that lay
ahead. "I would have trouble enough without having
the altitude to contend with." Indeed, at eight thou-

sand feet above sea level, the thinner air would have hampered even the most conditioned athlete.

"Besides," the Romanian added, "someone should stay back here to keep the equipment stabilized." He was seated between Shih Consai's prototype laser and his modification of the XT-22 warhead. Both weapons were strapped securely in place, but Hannas-ma had to concede the need to guard against any accidental jostling that might jar them from their moorings.

"Very well," he told Yurvi, shifting the Winnebago into drive. With a thousand fewer pounds to carry, the engine labored less tentatively and Hannas-ma was able to coax it to proceed up the mountain.

As they had during the attack on the Army train in Oregon, the members of the Yellow Brigade had disguised themselves as forest workers. And rather than toting conspicuous M-14s, the men had Beretta automatics secreted in shoulder holsters tucked beneath vests the same color as the bright traffic cones they set up across the firebreak.

Once the barricade was up and the sign had been put in place, Shih Consai and the others started uphill on foot. Jon Yang detoured to a nearby thicket, behind which he could hide while keeping an eye on the firebreak to ensure against anyone's stumbling upon the Brigade's dire mission.

A hundred yards ahead, Hannas-ma Yang pulled the Winnebago off the steep incline of the firebreak and onto a more level section of land. He pulled on the parking brake and left the engine running, then got out of the vehicle with Dr. Yurvi and surveyed the landscape. Twenty feet away, a locked, knee-high metallic box protruded from the weeds and lupine.

Hannas-ma knew that inside the box was a resistivity gauge installed by the United States Geological Survey two years ago. Unseen cables reached out from the gauge, connecting to high-tech prods embedded in the earth that measured variations in the electrical conductivity of the surrounding rock mass as well as changes in its density and the amount of water in the rock. This was but one of more than a dozen different types of instruments used throughout California in gathering crucial data for transmission to the Quakesim computers in Ventura. Elsewhere in this section of the Mammoth wilderness area were five more resistivity gauges and two gravimeters, which responded to the rise and fall of land and changes in underground rock density by sensing variations in local force of gravity. Long known as an area prone to both earthquakes and volcanic activity, the Mammoth Lakes region was the most meticulously monitored land mass in California aside from the primary fault systems running along the state's coastline.

When the others completed their hike and joined Hannas-ma and Dr. Yurvi, the group set about the task of pinpointing the exact location at which they wanted to prepare the nuclear charge. Pi Yung-lu, the oldest of the brigadiers, had a background in surveying, and after comparing the computer printouts of the area with a topographical map, he found his bearings and, with Shih Consai's help, took the necessary measurements.

"Here," he finally said, standing next to the designated area, which appeared to be nothing more than an inconsequential heap of forest debris. However, when the others came over and removed the refuse, they uncovered a half-buried metal box slightly larger than the one that held the resistivity gauge. Prying the lid off the box was no problem, and then the brigadiers found themselves staring at a round, doughnut-shaped plate, in the middle of which was a pry-off cap which Shih Consai removed to reveal a hole the width of his fist.

"Perfect," Consai whispered as he knelt down to inspect the orifice. "It's still in excellent condition."

"I'll get the van," Hannas-ma said.

Another of the raiders asked Shih what the hole was for and the scientist explained that it was originally intended for use as a site for a scintillation counter, yet another earthquake monitoring system in which a gauge was lowered down a deep shaft into a water well and calibrated to measure both water pressure and the amount of radon gas released into the water by strain on the surrounding bedrock.

"In this case, however," Shih concluded, "they misjudged the water table and drilled into solid ground. So you see, we already have a deep hole started, wide enough for the warhead. With the head start, it will take the laser only half the time and effort to penetrate deeply enough to where we can set off the charge without fear of radiation leaking to the surface."

"And that's important, yes?" Pi Yung-lu said.

"Quite," Shih divulged with an odd twinkle in his eyes. "We not only want to mask the fact that a bomb is responsible for what is about to happen, but we also want to ensure that we are not killed while setting it off."

"Of course," Pi murmured weakly.

Hannas-ma Yang returned to the Winnebago, which was parked some fifty yards away, and slowly negotiated the terrain to where Pi Yung-lu and the others were waiting. Once the vehicle was stopped, the rear doors were opened and the men carefully went about unstrapping the laser and the warhead, then carried them out in preparation for their use. Dr. Yurvi and Dr. Shih Consai supervised and the task was undertaken with the utmost care and precision.

"You are sure this is going to work?" Pi asked at one point.

Shih responded. "As sure as we can be until we actually try it out. That is why we are here in Mammoth and not nearer to the coast. If there are adjustments to be made, it's best that we make them before we tackle the San Andreas fault. That, after all, is our *real* objective."

FROM HIS VANTAGE POINT at the sentry post, all Jon Yang could see of his cohorts was a glint of sunlight bouncing off the chrome rack atop the Winnebago. A part of him wished that he was up there to see exactly how a device not much larger than an outboard motor could fire a laser ray capable of boring a deep hole into the earth like something out of one of the science fiction movies that had enthralled him as a child.

What Jon could clearly see from his perspective was a visually prominent fault scarp that undulated along the hilly terrain like a trail left by some gargantuan snake. From being around the two scientists for so long, he'd learned that such marks in the earth testified to recent quake activity and also signified an area still under stress from underground forces. It was likely that the coming quake would lengthen that scarp and perhaps even tear it open like an unhealed wound. By then, fortunately, he and the others would be far away from here, bound in the Winnebago for Tioga Pass and the scenic drive through Yosemite National Park on their way to the coast.

Jon's reverie was interrupted by the high-pitched whining of a car engine. It wasn't the Winnebago. He peered through the lower branches of his cover and saw a Jeep heading up the firebreak toward the barricade. Inside the vehicle were two bona fide uniformed park service employees.

Cursing under his breath, the sentry composed himself as best he could and emerged from cover, smiling and waving at the men in the Jeep.

"Morning," he called out.

"Morning," the driver said, pulling to a stop near the traffic cones and leaving the Jeep running as he read the posted sign. "Hmm, I don't remember hearing anything about this."

"It came up at the last minute," Jon explained, launching into the cover story he had prepared in the event of just such an emergency. "Apparently had some bears up here during the night nosing around the quake equipment. We're just putting the machines back on line and shoring up the barriers around them."

The passenger in the Jeep said, "Maybe we could help. I was always curious about how those machines worked."

"So am I," Jon said, "but they've got a special team on it, and they don't take too kindly to spec-

tators looking over their shoulders, if you know what
I mean.''

Both men in the Jeep looked long and hard at Jon,
sizing him up. Jon kept his smile and held his ground
during what seemed to be an interminable silence. Finally the driver sighed and shifted the Jeep into reverse.

''Well, that being the case, I guess we'll leave them
be,'' he told Jon. ''Have a good one.''

As the Jeep swung into reverse, Jon had a view of
the vehicle's dashboard and he saw the CB radio
mounted underneath it. The moment he saw the passenger reach for the radio's microphone, he knew that
the men hadn't been convinced by his story and were
about to call for verification. Jon couldn't allow that
to happen.

Reaching inside his vest, the brigadier pulled out his
Beretta 93-R and quickly dropped into a firing crouch.
With his left hand, he swung down a small grip affixed to the front of the trigger guard to aid his aim.
He had a 15-round magazine already in place, set to
fire 3-round bursts of 9 mm parabellum. Drawing
bead on the man with the mike, he pulled the trigger.

Five of the Beretta's first six shots peppered the
ranger's head and shoulder while the other took out
the windshield. Slain by the first shot, the man
dropped the mike and keeled over sharply to his right,
leaving behind a trail of blood and gore as he tumbled from the Jeep.

''James!'' Jon heard the driver yell to his companion as he slammed on the brakes. Stopping the Jeep

was the worst thing he could have done, however, because it made him a sitting target for the marksman behind him. Jon Yang only had to squeeze the trigger one more time to riddle the man's brains with a 3-round burst of high-velocity slugs. When the driver's foot slipped off the clutch, the Jeep bucked sharply forward, slamming him hard against the steering wheel before the engine stalled.

Lowering his weapon, Jon rushed forward to the Jeep and scanned the land around him to see if there was anyone nearby who might have witnessed the execution. He couldn't see anyone, but he was sure the sound of the gunshots had to have traveled for some distance. Fortunately, he was equally sure the shots would have echoed in so many directions that it would be difficult to trace them back to their actual source.

As he was dragging the slain passenger back to the Jeep, Jon Yang heard a noise behind him and saw Pi Yung-lu scrambling down the hillside with his Beretta drawn. Jon motioned that he had things under control and Pi put his gun away. As the two of them heaped the dead park workers into the back of the Jeep, the CB radio crackled to life.

"James, Malcolm." A woman's voice came over the radio's small speakers. "What's going on up your way? We thought we heard shots."

Both Pi and Jon stared at the radio, not sure what they should do.

"James, Malcolm, do you read me? Over."

Jon leaned across the front seat and picked up the mike, making sure that it wasn't turned on. He carefully replaced it in its cradle, then got behind the wheel of the Jeep and told Pi, "Hopefully she'll think they just strayed away from the Jeep for a few minutes."

Pi didn't look convinced. "If they heard shots and don't get an answer, they'll send someone to investigate."

Jon thought fast and started up the Jeep. As he revved the engine and began driving uphill toward his sentry post, he keyed the mike, holding it away from him so the engine's roar would help mask his voice. "Can't talk now," he said quickly. "Just scaring a bear away from a couple of hikers. Over and out."

Pi caught up with Jon after the Jeep was stashed in the brush. "I bought us maybe a couple more minutes at best," Jon said. "How close are they to being finished up there?"

"Soon, if all goes well," Pi said. "Shih says the old hole was still in good shape, so—"

His voice trailed off as they both heard the sound of the Winnebago starting down the hill. They moved aside the traffic cones long enough for the vehicle to drive past, then put the barricade back up and rejoined their companions.

"What was that shooting about?" Hannas-ma Yang asked as he glanced over at the Jeep. His brother quickly explained the situation with the park workers and the radio, then asked whether or not the bomb had been set.

"It goes off in just over an hour," Dr. Yurvi announced. His face, like that of Dr. Consai, was flushed with the excitement of one who has just seen a long-planned scheme put in motion.

"Plenty of time for us to put some miles behind us," Hannas-ma Yang said. "With any luck, no one will try to get in our way."

In case someone did attempt to stop the group, the other guerrillas were already breaking out their M-14s....

9

Montgomery Landlicott was not only on top of the roof, but he also felt on top of the world. For his part in the plutonium theft at the Cumberland Nuclear Research Center, he had received slightly more than $93,000, a princely sum that had readily thrown him into an alliance with Dr. Yurvi. He had big plans for the money. Fifty grand had already been turned over to a pair of human gorillas who'd come calling on him in Cumberland on behalf of a New Jersey loan shark, seeking repayment of money Landlicott had borrowed in a failed effort to ride out a run of bad luck at the blackjack tables in Atlantic City.

As for the rest of his take, he planned to help bankroll a major cocaine deal involving some old ex-Navy buddies up in Maine who regularly smuggled the white powder into the country on their lobster trawlers. By getting into the game at that point in the chain of distribution, he knew he could parlay his initial investment into a quarter of a million dollars by lining up the right dealers. One of the main reasons he was staying behind in Big Pine while most of the others were bound for the coast was that Landlicott had plans to return to Vegas the following day, where he would be introduced to Big Larry Zech, the syndicate's coke man on the main strip and provider of nose candy for any celebrity coming into town seeking a discreet toot to help deal with the razzle-dazzle.

And once he got that quarter mil?

A yacht. A sleek fifty-footer, loaded with enough provisions to last for weeks at a time so he could take to the wide blue waters and totally forget the rest of the world. He knew how to handle a boat that big, so he wouldn't have to bother hiring a crew. It'd be just him and some lean-legged blonde he'd lured away from a Vegas show bar. He'd take her along, party the time away those couple of weeks, then if he was tired of her he'd let her off when he reached port for more provisions and he'd go out and find himself a replacement. Once the money was running low, he'd take some time off to go ashore and cut himself in on another drug deal to replenish the kitty, then be off again.

"Gonna be sweet," he told himself. "Real sweet."

He was on the roof pulling more sentry duty. Two other brigadiers had remained behind to patrol the grounds in the event that something went wrong up in Mammoth Lakes and the men in the Winnebago had to retreat to Big Pine and plan an alternative strategy. If the mission in Mammoth went off without a hitch, Landlicott would be on his way to Vegas and the two guards would stay on as caretakers of the hatchery and its headquarters facilities for the Yellow River Brigade.

Of course, if all went well, the Brigade wouldn't be spending much more time in this backwater hide-away, Landlicott thought to himself as he dealt out another round of solitaire. Hell no. To hear Hannasma Yang tell it, after things fell into their places, the

Brigade would be heading overseas to take control of the Chinese government and handle their business from inside the walls of some sumptuous palace.

Yeah, sure, Landlicott mused, grinning to himself at the preposterousness of Hannas-ma's scenario. Shit, the odds were that sooner or later the whole Brigade would be rounded up by the Feds for their part in the Oregon bloodbath, and then they'd be either deep-sixed or else shuttled off to prison and forgotten about. By then Landlicott figured he'd be out on the Indian Ocean somewhere, far from even the longest arm of the law, banging the brains out of some sweet thing.

Landlicott was on a roll with the cards, ready to beat ol' Sol for the second time in a row, when he heard a faint drone in the distance. He didn't think much of it at first, but when the noise grew progressively louder and closer, he glanced up through the smoke of his cigarette and tried to pinpoint its location.

From the southeast, two small specks flew through the azure sky toward him. Before long they took on more shape, and Landlicott promptly shoved his cards aside in favor of high-powered binoculars. Within seconds of framing the approaching crafts and bringing them into focus, the man cursed under his breath.

They were both AH-64A Apaches, two-man Army choppers packing as deadly a punch as one was apt to find on any aircraft of their size and class. Landlicott had seen them at an air show in Maryland a couple of years ago, and even then the firepower they were equipped with had made an impression on him: eight Hellfire antitank missiles, thirty-eight 2.75-inch folding fin aerial rockets and twelve hundred rounds of 30 mm bullets with flare rockets. Their appearance on the horizon could mean only one thing, and Landlicott passed along the bad news by walkie-talkie to the two soldiers on the ground.

"We've been sniffed out," he said with grim calm. "You'd best find some cover and lay low. Make sure your first shots count 'cause you won't have the chance for seconds."

Grabbing his Stoner 63, Landlicott feverishly shifted interchangeable parts, opting for the submachine gun mode. No point screwing around with a wide spray of gunfire. He'd need one well-placed shot at a time to stand a chance against the invaders.

"Come on, baby," he whispered as the choppers drew closer and suddenly split off in separate directions, as if to assault the hatchery from opposite flanks. Landlicott kept his attention on the chopper to his left, for the simple reason that it would put the pilot into his sights when it went past . . . provided it did go past instead of coming head-on.

His strategy paid off, because as Landlicott tracked the Stoner to follow the flow of the copter, the man behind the controls of the Apache banked to the left, well within firing range, leaving himself clearly exposed to the 5.56 mm bullet that ripped through his side window and buried itself in his chest. The pilot instantly slumped to his right, dropping his hands from the controls and causing the chopper to immediately veer onto a collision course with the ground.

THE TWO HELICOPTERS had been pressed into service at Wisdom Plateau as the aircraft most capable of getting to the fish hatchery in the quickest time. And time was of the essence, especially once it had been determined that the Yellow River Brigade was more than likely on the verge of using the deadly arsenal it had put together over the past few days. Because the Apaches were two-seaters, there had been only room for one passenger to accompany each pilot. Kissinger and Schwarz had pulled rank to get the seats, and it was Gadgets who was riding in the Apache first targeted by Montgomery Landlicott.

Although Schwarz had never received any authorized flight training, he'd ridden alongside Jack Grimaldi enough times to have familiarized himself with some of the more basic skills of helicopter navigation. Now that his pilot was dead, Schwarz had no choice but to put his meager knowledge to use. And quickly. Given the awesome load of firepower the copter was toting, Gadgets knew that if they crashed the resulting explosion would deliver him into the next world as little more than an obliterated mass of charred ash. Worse yet, if indeed there were atomic weapons stored at the hatchery, the downed Apache could well set off a chain reaction that would blow Big Pine and half of Owens Valley off the map.

With split-second reflexes, Schwarz grabbed at the controls and tried to stabilize the runaway copter, which was already dipping sharply to one side, bringing the rotors dangerously close to the uppermost branches of the tall cottonwoods. When he overcompensated for the tilt, Gadgets almost flipped the Apache over, and the dead pilot slammed into him, further obstructing his efforts.

And as if these hindrances weren't enough, Schwarz heard more shattering glass to his right and realized he'd come within inches of taking the sniper's second shot in the head. The bullet burrowed into the cockpit ceiling, having taken out a monitoring light.

"I thought these windows were supposed to be bulletproof," Schwarz muttered to himself as he continued to fight with the controls. By some miracle he'd managed to veer away from the stand of cottonwoods and was now flying over a partial clearing. The chopper leveled off somewhat, and once he got a better feel for the collective pitch stick, Schwarz was able to finally tame the rotors, slowing their frantic whir enough so that the Apache descended, however jerkily.

Deliberately setting the craft down away from the clearing, Schwarz was able to use the dense bordering foliage to help break the less than graceful force of the landing. Touching ground with a jolting thud, Schwarz bounced in his seat and closed his eyes, bracing for the anticipated deafening roar of a crash-detonated Hellfire missile or ruptured fuel tank that would herald his instantaneous cremation. Neither occurred, however, and as he killed the Apache's engines, Schwarz realized that, at least for the time being, he had once again cheated the Reaper.

Covered with the slain pilot's blood, Schwarz glanced out at the terrain, plotting his next move as he used the downed chopper's radio to call the second Apache and report that his pilot was dead. The other pilot acknowledged the disclosure with a perfunctory grunt and passed along the bad news that backup forces were still a few minutes away from the scene.

Add to that the fact that the remaining copter couldn't use its full offensive capabilities because of the nuclear threat on the premises, and the outlook was decidedly bleak.

"Well, what the hell," Schwarz whispered to himself, glancing out at the clear blue sky. "As nice a day to die as any."

But if Death had Gadget's number, Schwarz had no intention of twiddling his thumbs waiting for the end. He'd go down the way he lived, pedal to the metal, giving no quarter. Once the other Apache touched down long enough to allow John Kissinger to disembark, Schwarz sized up the situation. Two ground soldiers and one handicapped chopper against whatever security force the Yellow River Brigade might have at its disposal.

"You've seen worse odds, Schwarz," Gadgets cheered himself as he readied for combat. Like every member of Able Team, he was packing an M-1911 Government Model automatic. The Colt-made .45, long a mainstay among United States enforcement agencies, had been retooled slightly by John Kissinger to better serve in the team's arsenal. Schwarz lowered its fold-down lever and, as Jon Yang had done with his Beretta up in the hills of Mammoth, Gadgets opted for a two-hand grip on the weapon, which sported a blunt suppressor to make its delivery of semiautomatic fire as noiseless as possible.

As he bailed out of the Apache, Schwarz drew more rifle fire from the roof of the hatchery and was forced to dive forward into the brush. Brittle limbs snapped under his weight and he felt the sting of smaller branches against his face. He continued to lie low several seconds longer, then rose to a partial crouch and peered in the direction of the hatchery. He could see Landlicott perched in the sniper's nest, now looking off in another direction, no doubt trying to draw bead on Kissinger. Schwarz took that for a good sign, since if there were more than one sniper, most likely he would still be under fire.

Taking advantage of Landlicott's divided attention, Schwarz scrambled through the foliage and broke into a huddled run across the clearing, hoping to circle in closer to the hatchery while using the cottonwoods for cover. He was a few yards from the amber-leaved trees when he suddenly froze.

Fifteen feet ahead of him, one of the Yellow River Brigade sentries was staring at him over the sights of his M-14. During that split second that Gadgets Schwarz's instincts had failed him, leaving him a still target, the brigadier pulled the trigger.

JOHN KISSINGER HEARD the chatter of the M-14, but the dense flora prevented him from tracing its trajectory to the man who had fired it. Because the chopper that had dropped him off was now on the other side of the grounds, Cowboy knew that the obvious target of the rifle's blasts had to be Schwarz. Much as he might have wanted to lend assistance to his cohort, Kissinger had been through hellfire enough times to know that when one set out on a mission, the mission was top priority at all times and at all costs. His mission was to get to the hatchery and make sure that if a nuclear arsenal was present no one was going to be foolish enough to trigger it.

And it wasn't as if Kissinger didn't have to dance clear of his own share of enemy gunfire. The sniper on the roof had apparently reassembled his Stoner to its belt-fed machine gun mode, and a steady stream of 5.56 mm fire chewed threw the oleander and other brush that was providing Kissinger with a flimsy cover.

Although he had his Colt automatic in his shoulder holster, Kissinger had thrown himself into the fray with a heavier piece of artillery. His Armbrust Disposable looked like the unlikely cross between a bazooka and a dulcimer, but the kind of music it made wasn't pretty. Essentially a portable antitank weapon, the Armbrust fired its powerful sealed rounds with surprising discretion, using firing pistons at each end of its main tube to seal in flash and gases, thereby reducing noise. The weapon also had a countermass of plastic flakes that helped buffer recoil. Although Kissinger knew that the Armbrust had a range of nearly 1500 meters, he wanted to get as close as he could to the hatchery before using it, for the same reason that the chopper was obliged to hold back from uncorking a Hellfire missile that could have easily reduced the main building to rubble.

Keying his walkie-talkie, Kissinger asked the Apache's pilot to make a high pass over the hatchery and get a good look at the sniper's nest. "Keep him busy and try to see if he's got one of those XT-22s up with him," he added.

"Roger."

As the Apache swept wide and prepared its approach, Kissinger cocked his head to one side, realizing that he hadn't heard a second round of fire from the M-14 off near the cottonwoods. He was partially relieved, because although there was a chance Schwarz had dropped the man who had fired it, the rifle's silence could just as easily mean it had taken out its target, in which case Kissinger could expect to have company in the not-too-distant future.

The helicopter drew in on the sniper with its 30 mm guns firing, an adequate enough response to keep the man on the roof pinned behind the barricades of his nest. Kissinger broke into a run at the sound of the first blasts, taking long strides toward the hatchery, yet also zigzagging in a manner reminiscent of his glory days as a wide receiver for the Ohio State Buckeyes and Cleveland Browns. That had been nearly twenty years ago, so he might have lost a step or two, but his reflexes were still finely honed. When he was suddenly surprised by the appearance of a ground sentry lunging out from the oleander with a bayonet affixed to the end of his M-14, Kissinger used his instincts and forward momentum to keep the brigadier from impaling him. With one fluid motion, he deflected the thrust of the bayonet with the flat shoulder brace of the Armbrust, then body-slammed his smaller foe with the full brunt of his two hundred pounds.

The two men went down hard, but Kissinger was on top and in control from the onset. He landed with one knee driving sharply into the sentry's upper thigh and his free forearm clipping the man's clavicle. The brigadier dropped his M-14, howling in pain, and feebly attempted to claw at Kissinger's face with his long, slender fingers. Cowboy tucked his head in close to his shoulders and leaned on the antitank weapon, which he'd laid across the enemy's throat. He felt fingers tearing at his hair, groping for his ears, but he kept his concentration on the Armbrust, and soon he could feel the other man's strength ebbing. The sentry made a few choking, gasping sounds, fighting to pull in air through his strangled windpipe, but it was a losing battle and the man was dead even before Kissinger's brute strength broke his neck.

Perspiring freely from the brief skirmish, Kissinger rolled off his victim, wondering if this was the same man who had shot at Schwarz. He had little time for such speculation, as his walkie-talkie came alive with news from the Apache.

"No nukes on the roof," the pilot told him. "I almost nailed him myself but I'll leave him for you."

"Roger," Kissinger said. "I'm close enough to take the whole nest out now. Just keep him preoccupied."

As the Apache banked again and flew close to the hatchery, Kissinger moved to the edge of a clearing and knelt on one knee, bracing the Armbrust against his shoulder. Besides the 67 mm warhead already inside the tube, he had another three rounds clipped to his waist, but Kissinger wanted to make the first shot count. Although this weapon wasn't from the Stony Man arsenal and lacked the modifications Kissinger had made on the team's Armbrusts to improve their accuracy, he still felt confident he could keep the blast confined to the roof.

As he was about to pull the trigger, Kissinger detected motion out of the corner of his eye. Reflexively he swung the Armbrust around. At such close range, one shot would carry enough wallop to rip a man's torso away from his limbs. Cowboy didn't demonstrate such grisly possibilities, because he instantly recognized the approaching figure and held back from firing.

Gadgets Schwarz rushed to Kissinger's side, glancing down at the fallen guardsman.

"I ran into one of those, too," Gadgets said. "Put a bullet in my walkie-talkie before I could take him out."

"Glad you made it," Kissinger said, turning his attention back to the hatchery. "Now let's get a move on before we lose another chopper."

Cowboy realigned his sights on the sniper's nest, where Montgomery Landlicott was taking potshots at the Apache. When Kissinger fired, the Armbrust made less noise than the Stoner. Without so much as a telltale flash or puff of smoke, the launched warhead took less than two seconds to reach its destination.

With a resounding explosion, the roof atop the hatchery's main building trembled, and shrapnel flew wildly from what had once been the fortified lair of Landlicott's sniper nest. The gunman was now visible, lying near his disabled Stoner, howling in pain and twitching spasmodically from the wounds he'd sustained. Given the directness of the hit, it was a miracle that he was alive, much less in one piece.

When there was no further show of gunfire from the enemy, Kissinger and Schwarz made a mad dash for the hatchery, both toting their Government Models. Behind them, the Apache was touching down in the parking lot, and off in the distance the rumble of a much larger CH-47 Chinook announced the overdue arrival of reinforcements.

"Cavalry's a little late to save the day this time," Kissinger told Schwarz as they closed in on the buildings.

"What the hell, we always were glory hogs," Gadgets quipped. "Look, I'll take the doorway here. You get the back. Ten count. Ten...nine..."

The two men split up. Schwarz pinned himself against the nearest entrance to the main building, counting down silently as he readied his Colt. When he reached zero, he lunged through the opening half-crouched, veering sharply to one side in case there were ambushers within. Encountering no resistance, he moved down the hallway and regrouped with Kissinger in the main laboratory, which still held most of the paraphernalia used by Dr. Yurvi and Dr. Shih Consai. It didn't take them long to take a quick inventory of the place and realize the bottom line.

"Seems like we closed down the corral after the horses got away," Schwarz said.

Kissinger looked over the schematic diagrams on the chalkboard and nodded grimly. "Yeah, and from the looks of it, they've got the XT-22s armed and modified for use with some kind of laser drilling system."

Schwarz frowned. "Wait a minute. That's what Shih Consai was working on when he deep-sixed."

Kissinger went over to one of the workbenches and began leafing through research notes, some of them scribbled in Chinese, some of them written on pads with Shih's letterhead. "If he died, his ghost is up here working overtime."

"Shit, I don't like the way this is shaping up."

"Join the club," Kissinger said, heading toward an open doorway. "Here's the stairs to the roof. Let's hope that poor bastard up there's got a little life and a loose tongue left in him."

The men bounded up the steps, pushing open a trapdoor that led to the flattened roof. The Apache pilot had already come over and put a hose to use, wetting down the spot fires started by the Armbrust. He directed his spray away from Schwarz and Kissinger as they made their way to the wounded sniper.

Montgomery Landlicott was in a state of giddy shock, laughing strangely as he looked up at the man responsible for his condition. If he knew that his right leg had been severed just below the knee, Landlicott showed no signs of minding aside from the wild look of pain in his eyes and the feverish stream of sweat pouring from his brow.

"Get me to the yacht!" he cackled. "Get me to the yacht and I'll be okay!"

"Where did they go?" Schwarz demanded, crouching near the sniper. "And when?"

Blood gurgled up through Landlicott's lips, and he spit red as he howled, "Get me out on the deep blue sea, Mama!"

Schwarz slapped the man's face with the flat of his hand, trying to snap him out of his hysteria. It worked. Landlicott recoiled and fell silent a moment. His breath was labored and there was a rattling in his lungs, no doubt attributable to the shrapnel he'd taken in the chest. Kissinger knelt close by and tried as best he could to stanch the flow of blood from the stump of the man's severed leg. Fifty yards away, the monstrous Chinook floated down near the Apache, raising a rotor wash so strong that some of the less rootbound weeds began tumbling across the parched terrain. A bay door opened and armed soldiers poured out onto the parking lot, ready to do battle with an enemy that had already been neutralized.

"We'll get you help," Schwarz bartered with Landlicott, "but first you have to tell us where they went."

With monumental effort, Landlicott raised one hand and pointed north. "Mahhhh…Mammoth…"

Before the interrogation could proceed any further, there was a new rumbling that drowned out even the roar of the Chinook's twin rotors. The building beneath the men on the roof began to sway as if it had suddenly been given a life of its own. Schwarz and Kissinger looked at each other with apprehension and realization.

"Earthquake!" the Apache pilot shouted from the ground, dropping his hose and running clear of the building.

As the ground continued to shake with increasing intensity, Kissinger and Schwarz both lost their balance and felt themselves being bounced about on the roof like jacks being tossed by a child. It was all either man could do to roll with the quake's flow and work their way to the edge, then push off. It was almost a twenty-foot drop, and the fact that the men were off balance made the fall even more precarious. Relying on their limited paratrooper training, Kissinger and Schwarz tried as best they could to land feetfirst and roll on impact, but the fact that the ground itself was moving thwarted their timing. Kissinger managed a reasonably pain-free landing, but Schwarz, whose ankles were still tender from a mountain climbing incident several months back, could feel sharp jolts of pain run up his legs the moment he touched down, and once he stopped moving he knew that he'd just undone some of the past weeks of healing.

But at least he was alive, which was more than could be said for Montgomery Landlicott, who had disappeared from view as the weakened roof of the hatchery collapsed inward. Elsewhere, massive holding tanks splashed water and fish onto land, and those few receptacles located above ground ruptured at the seams, flooding the grounds with water and frantic trout.

The Chinook took back to the air, where the quake had no effect on it, but the men who had already disembarked could be seen straggling about the parking lot like drunks, caught up in the grip of the tremor. For more than a minute and a half, the ground continued to pitch and roll in full frenzy, pulling down more and more of the poorly constructed main building and its adjacent stations. The half-hidden satellite dish broke loose and wobbled back and forth on its sides. Both Apache copters tipped on their sides and were propped up only by rotor blades biting into the dirt.

And then, as quickly as it had begun, the quake ceased. There was a still, almost unreal silence on the grounds, followed soon after by the mutterings of the soldiers who had been subjected to the earth's whimsy.

"They've done it," Kissinger said aloud, looking to the north. "Those assholes started a quake."

"They sure did," Schwarz said, grimacing through his pain. "And something tells me we better get to safe ground as soon as we can, 'cause we're going to be riding out some mean aftershocks any minute."

10

On the DC-10 taking Aaron Kurtzman and 154 other passengers to California, the in-flight movie had been the latest James Bond escapade. Kurtzman hadn't bothered renting a headset for the flick, and although he was sitting only a few rows back from the screen in the first-class section of the plane, he rarely glanced up for more than a few seconds of diversion. After all, Stony Man Farm's chief communications expert lived and breathed the same air of gizmo-laden espionage and global intrigue that was the stuff of Bond movies, only in Kurtzman's case he was a team player embroiled in ongoing plots in which there was no scriptwriter standing on the sidelines to ensure that the outcome would always be rosy.

A good case in point was the attack on Stony Man Farm several years ago, in which some of the organization's own security people had abetted marauders who had stormed the compound. Kurtzman had been paralyzed below the waist from a bullet to the spine before the enemy had been neutralized. And as for the men of Able Team whom he now supported from the confines of a wheelchair, it was not their enviable lot to go into battle wearing smirks and tuxedos and emerge unscathed after protracted, prop-happy chase sequences. No, more often than not the men donned camous and Kevlar jackets, yet still found themselves scarred and wounded following skirmishes that were swift and brutal rather than drawn-out and spiced with comic relief.

And so, as James Bond treated the other passengers to a glamorized view of derring-do, Kurtzman devoted the bulk of his attention to the more menial task of familiarizing himself with schematic diagrams and tech manuals dealing with the operation of the Quakesim HO-29 seismological monitoring system in Ventura. Lesser souls were afforded the luxury of a four-month training regimen geared specifically to the HO-29 before even being allowed near the complex quake-monitoring mainframes. Kurtzman had a little less than five hours.

As those five hours ended and the jumbo jet set down on the runway in Ventura, the Bear—so nicknamed for an imposing physique he still maintained through vigorous conditioning, despite his partial paralysis—felt that he'd had an adequate enough overview of the Quakesim's computers to roll up his sleeves and do what he could to get the system back on line.

As he wheeled himself off the plane, Kurtzman scanned the crowd waiting inside the terminal for new arrivals. He hadn't been told who would be picking him up, and with Schwarz and Kissinger up north, he had no real expectation of spotting a familiar face. Accordingly, he was suitably stunned when his diminutive former associate broke away from the others and walked toward him.

"Lao Ti!" Kurtzman exclaimed. "What on earth . . . ?"

"Hello, Aaron," the woman told him, smiling broadly. "I take it somebody forgot to mention I was back."

"You're right," Kurtzman admitted. "And I have to admit, it's a very pleasant surprise. You're looking well."

They traded small talk as they went to the baggage claim area. Thanks to his connections and a well-placed phone call, Kurtzman's luggage and powerized wheelchair were the first things to be unloaded from the DC-10, and after he transferred from the manual chair the airline had provided, he and Lao Ti left for the parking lot, where she had secured the use of a van designed for the use of the disabled, with hydraulic lifts to hoist the Bear into the vehicle.

Once they were on their way to the Quakesim facility, Kurtzman patted the tech manuals for the HO-29. "We have our work cut out for us, I'm afraid."

"You're right on that count," Lao Ti said. "I've been working all morning with the team that's troubleshooting the system, and we're still only cracking the tip of the iceberg."

"Sounds worse than I thought."

"The big problem is the saboteurs didn't just throw a monkey wrench into the works," Lao Ti explained. "If that had been the case, we might have been able to just slap in replacement components and bring things back on line. What they did was rework a lot of the circuitry in ways that avoid detection during standard benchmark tests. It's like a maze. We think we're onto something and it turns out to be a dead end."

"Sounds like someone familiar with the whole system," Kurtzman observed. "I take it someone's investigating along those lines?"

"FBI," Lao Ti said. "Naturally, the first thought was that it might have been an inside job carried out by some people on the night shift, but except for a guard out front, they were all downed with Tasers and given injections that put them out until the work was all done."

"Doesn't sound too promising."

"No, it doesn't," Lao Ti said. "The Bureau's doing checks on all personnel at the site, and they're also branching out to the companies that did the manuals and handled the manufacturing of parts. I think I heard them say that angle alone gives them more than three thousand suspects, so it's apt to be slow going.

"As for the NOWAR people, they've all volunteered to take polygraphs or whatever it takes to prove they weren't involved. The feeling is they're on the level, especially now that we've got the lead on the Yellow River Brigade."

"The who?"

"Oh, it must have come up after you were on the plane." Lao Ti went on to explain about the recent investigative breakthrough up at Wisdom Plateau and how the Chinese terrorist band had been linked with the sabotage of that facility's monitoring station as well as the theft of the XT-22 warheads. When she divulged the going theory that all the group's recent activities were geared toward possible attempts to trigger earthquakes in California, Kurtzman let out a long breath.

"Could anyone really be that desperate?" he wondered aloud, already knowing the answer.

They rode silently for a while. Lao Ti was driving parallel to the coastline. It was a beautiful day, and although only a few brave souls were out in the chilly autumn waters of the Pacific, the beach was speckled with Californians taking advantage of one last chance to work on their tans.

Suddenly the van began to veer and lurch about on the freeway. Lao Ti grappled with the steering wheel, trying to regain control over the vehicle.

"Flat tire?" Kurtzman asked.

"No," Lao Ti responded, finally braking the van. "Look!"

Elsewhere on the freeway, traffic had ground to a sudden halt, and the reason soon became obvious, as the van continued to shake even after it had come to a complete stop.

"Oh, no..." Kurtzman muttered, fearing the worst.

Like the other motorists, he and Lao Ti stayed put until several seconds after the tremor had passed. Even then, when the cars proceeded forward, they did so slowly, as if expecting to stop again any moment.

"It's happened," Lao Ti whispered, her face ashen. "They actually did it."

"It was fairly mild here," Kurtzman said. "I wonder how close we were to the epicenter?"

"We'll find out soon enough," Lao Ti said, turning off the freeway and driving past Truckers' Heaven toward the Quakesim facility.

AS HE EXPECTED, Mel Bronson was put back to work almost immediately after being questioned about the raid on the earthquake monitoring station. As one of the programmers and maintenance people most familiar with the HO-29, he was too valuable to be left out of the effort to put the Quakesim system back on line. Bronson also knew that it was likely he and the other personnel who had been knocked out might still be watched closely for evidence of complicity with the sabotage, and he'd taken great pains to plot a strategy for assuring others of his reliability while at the same time ensuring that he could keep the computers' in-house monitoring capabilities compromised for the next forty-eight hours.

During the two hours he'd had to tamper with the Quakesim mainframes the night before, Bronson had painstakingly rigged numerous hard-to-trace glitches in the circuitry; these could be subsequently repaired in such a way as to give the appearance that they were steps in the right direction as far as restoring the HO-29 to full working order, when in fact, the triggered chain of commands would run the Quakesim data banks through a high-tech runaround. Essentially, Bronson's diabolical wizardry allowed him to take credit for every step forward that he initiated and to avoid any association with the two steps backward that cropped up elsewhere in the system soon afterward. The others on the emergency crew looked on him as a key player in the race to fix the computer, when the fact was that every minute he was allowed to tinker with the Quakesim he was actually being given more control over its disability.

Bronson was at work on the interfacing cables that linked the monolithic, submerged replica of the state of California with the input mainframe when he heard the unmistakable grinding sound of the simulated tectonic plates. A low-pitched siren mounted to the framework of the water tank began to sound in short staccato bursts, signaling that somewhere in the state a quake surpassing a 5.0 Richter reading had just taken place.

They did it, Bronson thought to himself as he immediately backed away from the coils and bounded up a wrought-iron ladder to a scaffolding that ran above the state replica. Several other technicians had already reached the landing, and Bronson joined them in looking down at the tank. Diodes representing every monitoring machine throughout the state dotted the replica like an acupuncturist's needles, and these machines now registering abnormal seismic readings blinked at intervals that corresponded to the intensity of the quake in their vicinity. The shorter the intervals between blinks, the closer the station was to the quake. Those diodes that didn't blink at all but rather glowed steadily marked the vicinity of the tremor's epicenter.

"Mammoth," a woman called out from the other end of the scaffolding. "It's coming out of Mammoth Lakes."

Bronson recognized the voice and glanced up, seeing Rona Lynne for the first time, though she'd arrived in Ventura with Lao Ti an hour before. In fact, he hadn't seen his wife in more than four months. They acknowledged each other uncertainly, caught off guard, and before they could do anything else, they were distracted by the sudden trembling beneath them.

More alarms sounded throughout the facility and people instinctively took the practiced precautions of seeking cover. Those trapped on the landing, however, could only grab hold of the railing and ride out the tremors.

The diodes on the replica dramatically demonstrated the way that a quake's force emanated outward from its point of origin. As was natural, Ventura being more than three hundred miles from Mammoth Lakes, the shock waves were much less severe than those felt in most areas farther inland. Accordingly, the trembling lasted only a few seconds, and the diodes poking up from the HO-29's simulated Ventura coastline pulsed in a much slower rhythm than those representing places like Fresno, Bakersfield and Visalia. If anything, the overall visual effect most closely resembled the way ripples sweep out in concentric circles around a pebble dropped in a pond.

Once the first tremor had passed, the alarms were shut off and reset as the technicians scurried about with renewed frenzy, trying to see what sort of information the Quakesim might pass along to the monitoring systems. It quickly became obvious, however, that although the HO-29 was sending out recording data, none of it was being routed through the in-house configuration. Instead, all the information was processed by the satellite transmission system that normally sent duplicate records to Wisdom Plateau. Because of the sabotage, those transmitted signals were being sent somewhere into space that was not in the path of any orbiting American satellite.

"This is maddening!" Bronson exclaimed, coaxing as much indignation as he could into his voice. For added emphasis he slammed his fist against the wall next to the unresponsive computer bank he was standing near. He'd pulled the punch at the last second, but acted as if he'd hit the wall full force.

"Take it easy, Mel," one of his co-workers told him. "We need you on this, okay?"

"I can't help it," he said with feigned frustration. "Shit, all this info's slipping right through our fingers like sand!"

"You keep pounding walls and your fingers will swell so much nothing will be able to slip through them," Rona said as she came over to her estranged husband. "George is right. You can't let this get the better of you."

"Sure thing, nurse," Bronson deadpanned. "Whatever you say."

There was a moment of awkward silence between them, then Rona said, "I heard what happened to you. Are you okay?"

"Yeah," Bronson muttered. "I'm fine. What brings you here, anyway? I know you didn't come all this way on my account."

"I'm here for the same reason you are, Mel," Rona explained. "It's vital that we get the Quakesim back on line as soon as possible."

"Gee, no kidding."

"Let's not bare our fangs in public, okay?" Rona said.

Bronson shrugged. "Suit yourself."

A second, milder tremor rolled through the facility, setting off the alarms again. Rona and Bronson were jostled into each other, the first time they'd touched since their separation. She quickly pulled away, her face red with embarrassment.

"I'm apt to be here awhile," she told him. "How about if we call a truce for the time being, okay?"

"Fine by me," Bronson said. "It wasn't my idea to break up in the first place, remember?"

"Let's not get into that."

Bronson nodded and started off, calling over his shoulder, "See you around."

Rona watched him walk away, wondering sadly to herself how their once happy marriage could have deteriorated so rapidly. She was well aware that sometimes people changed in ways that took them in different directions, but Mel's transformation had seemed unnaturally abrupt. By the time she'd asked for a separation, she'd come to feel that he was a complete stranger to her, almost as if at one point an impostor had taken the place of the man she'd married. Why had it happened? She wondered if she'd ever find out.

She put aside her musings when she saw Lao Ti enter the facility with Aaron Kurtzman. Walking over to join them, Rona was introduced to the wizard, who marveled at his first glimpse of the enormous Quakesim.

"It's amazing, it looks even bigger than I imagined," he said. "How'd it fare during the shaker?"

"It's operating fine," Rona answered. "It's just that all its data's lost in space somewhere. We can sort of eyeball what's happening from the landing, but until we can get some solid in-house readings, there's not much we can do here as far as making predictions is concerned."

"But you have the lowdown on this quake?" Kurtzman asked.

"Not totally," Rona said. "All we can tell from here is that the epicenter was around Mammoth Lakes and that from the emanation pattern it was probably somewhere near a six. For specifics we'll have to wait for calls from the field. Cal Tech will have something, and so will Colorado. As a matter of fact, I think I'd like to check on it right now."

"Go ahead, please," Kurtzman said. Once Rona had left, he turned to Lao Ti. "I want to try to intercept the guys back East. They're scheduled to be flying into L.A., but given what's happened, I think it'd be better for them to divert to Mammoth. Schwarz and Kissinger might need some help up there."

"I just hope they're okay," Lao Ti murmured. "Mammoth's too close to Wisdom Plateau and Big Pine for coincidence. If this quake was set off by a bomb, that means they didn't get to the Brigade in time. Or if they did . . ."

"Show me where I can use a phone and I'll try to get through to them," Kurtzman said.

Lao Ti nodded and led the way past the laboring crews. Kurtzman powered himself along on his motorized cart, surveying the facility.

Mel Bronson watched them from the console he'd just gone to work on. Turning to the man next to him, he asked, "You know anything about those two over there?"

The other man glanced in the direction Bronson had gestured. "The lady's here with the Chinese delegation cozying up to the folks in Pasadena," he muttered with obvious distaste. "I overheard her saying something about having ties with some hotshot special forces group back East. Could be the guy in the chair's part of that team. Lot of good they're going to do.''

"Yeah," Bronson said, turning back to his work. "Yeah.''

11

Oleg Levdroko stared out at the diamond glitter of sunlight bounding off the waves of Monterey Bay. In the five years he'd been serving at the San Francisco desk of the KGB's First Department of the Foreign Directorate, he'd only made this southern trek four times, and in each instance he'd been overwhelmed by the coastal area's beauty, with its rugged pines, abundant flora and the cobalt-blue waters that threw themselves against the untamed shoreline. As on the previous three trips, Levdroko vowed to himself that he would have to come this way more often. It was important to get out of the city, if only to give his nerves a brief respite from the pressures of his job.

Levdroko switched on a radio that poured classical music into the rear compartment of the limousine. A Chopin recital. Too boisterous. He reached for the control panel and pressed a button to seek out the next station. Along this stretch of coastline the reception was poor, however, and the only other signal the Russian could pull in was that of a news channel. Levdroko stayed tuned, certain that the recent quake would soon be discussed.

He was right.

Measuring 6.8 on the Richter scale, the Mammoth-based quake had wreaked considerable havoc throughout central California, triggering countless landslides, cracking roadways and temporarily disrupting the flow of water to the south due to damage to the Los Angeles Aqueduct. Innumerable buildings and homes in Mammoth, Bishop and neighboring communities sustained the most destruction, although the quake was responsible for minor damage as far as 350 miles from its epicenter. The death toll thus far was seventeen, with injuries running into the hundreds. No estimate had been put on monetary losses as yet, but the figure was expected to approach or surpass the two-hundred-million-dollar mark attributed to the 1987 Whittier Narrows quake near Los Angeles.

Lastly, and most important in Levdroko's mind, there was no mention in the news of any abnormal activities being responsible for the tremor, which scientists claimed was the strongest felt in California in the past five years. The Russian was naturally concerned that investigators might turn up evidence that a nuclear charge had been responsible for triggering the quake. Since the Mammoth tremor was essentially only a trial run in a far larger master plan the KGB had played a key role in, it was important that no suspicions be aroused, that no connection be made between the quake and recent terrorist activities perpetrated both on the West Coast and in West Virginia.

When the news shifted to mention of the latest troubles on Wall Street, Levdroko switched back to the classical music station, where Chopin had given way to a soothing piece by Joseph Haydn. The Russian eased back in the plush embrace of the limo's leather seat and mulled over this, the most daring of exploits he had undertaken since the KGB had placed him in command of the much coveted San Francisco desk.

The scope of this new mission was massive, and proportionally fraught with risk, but Levdroko had been forced to such drastic measures after the recent debacle in San Diego, where his handpicked operative, Sergei Karanov, had failed miserably in his attempts to infiltrate and compromise the United States military effort in that area through the use of prostitutes and mind-control drugs. The bungling of that effort and Karanov's subsequent desertion had resulted in an ultimatum being delivered to Levdroko from his superiors in Moscow. Either the San Francisco desk would produce some significant results, and soon, or else there would be a new head of that branch. The implied threat was that if such action proved necessary, Levdroko's own head would roll, perhaps literally as well as figuratively.

And so Oleg Levdroko had stepped up the timetable for his master plan. He had already laid the groundwork over recent years, infiltrating various American facilities with KGB personnel and winning over several high-ranking figures, including Dr. Robert Yurvi. If it had been allowed to be carried out at the originally projected pace, Levdroko's plan would not have reached its present stage for another two years. However, the call from Moscow had placed a priority on expediency, and therefore Levdroko had been forced to seek out an ally to help speed up the timetable, preferably an easily deceived zealot whose personal agenda could be milked for the needs of the KGB. In Hannas-ma Yang and the Yellow River Brigade, Levdroko had found the perfect pawns. A few insinuated promises, the outlay of some working capital and some behind-the-scenes assistance was all that Levdroko had to put forth to make the Yellow River Brigade a goon squad willing to carry out the dirty work necessary to implement the plan that already involved the input of Yurvi and certain key figures in the XT-22 missile program.

And so far things were working out nicely. Although Levdroko would have preferred a more subtle theft of the XT-22s in Oregon, Hannas-ma's men had gotten the job done. Although the Mammoth quake had been .2 tamer than the 7.0 jolt predicted by Yurvi and Shih Consai, it seemed clear that it was possible to use scientific and military technology to unleash the earth's potential fury in order to fulfill a predetermined objective of making strategic gains based on the resulting destruction.

Rounding the southernmost bend of the bay, the limousine turned off the freeway onto Monterey Peninsula and the famed Seventeen Mile Drive that wound past multimillion-dollar estates and several world-class golf courses, including Pebble Beach. Halfway along the stretch, Levdroko's chauffeur, Wilhelm, used a cellular phone to call ahead so that when he reached the driveway, the imposing wrought-iron gates slowly parted. He was able to drive onto the grounds of a sprawling fifteen-acre site covering rolling terrain and surrounded by sweeping Monterey pines and a high-security fence of stone and barbed wire.

Atop a knoll with a view of the Pacific was the main house, a two-story, twelve-room wooden structure erected half a century ago and based on a design by Frank Lloyd Wright. Originally owned by a cannery baron and onetime drinking partner of John Steinbeck, the estate had passed through several hands over the past decades and was now property of a shadow corporation owned by the KGB. Levdroko had been behind the acquisition, favoring the site not only as a safehouse for Russian operatives and a training base for espionage agents, but also as a gathering place where high-placed spies could socialize with important figures living along the famed Drive and in nearby Carmel or Pacific Grove. As far as the world was concerned, this was solely the home of United States businessman and entrepreneur Lyle Evertt, a man with a penchant for lavish parties and political fund-raisers that put him in touch with some of the nation's most influential figures. Evertt's status as a KGB agent was a well-kept secret, and during supposedly confidential conversations held within the walls of the mansion, the man had loosened the tongue of many a confidant, thereby supplying the Soviets with a unique perspective on the inner workings of America's power elite.

Today, however, Evertt was overseas on yet another of his extended vacations, and the estate was set aside for other tasks. When the limousine finally reached the end of the quarter-mile-long driveway, it pulled to a stop next to a Winnebago layered with the dust of several states. Hannas-ma Yang and his brother Jon were sitting out on a nearby porch, dining on Cantonese takeout food and enjoying the midday sun.

"Congratulations," Levdroko said as he stepped out of the limousine and joined the two men. He took great pains not to betray his feelings of smug superiority over the revolutionaries. As always, he made sure that they felt they were peers, equals joined by common goals. "Thanks to you," he told them, "it looks as if our dreams will soon be close at hand."

"Let us hope so," Hannas-ma said.

"So, tell me," Levdroko said after he shook both men's hands. "Were there any complications?"

"Nothing we couldn't overcome." Jon Yang went on to explain about the inopportune arrival of the park service employees while the nuclear charge was being readied in the hills near Mammoth Lakes. When Levdroko heard the two men had been gunned down and left at the site, his face turned stony. There was no way he could suppress his concern or anger.

"You should have brought the bodies," he told the brothers coldly.

"Why?" Hannas-ma Yang had picked up on the Russian's changed mood and rose to the challenge, setting aside his chopsticks and meeting Levdroko's gaze directly.

"Because now the officials have had their suspicions aroused," Levdroko said. "I just heard the news about the quake and there was no mention of any killings. That can only mean one thing, that they are holding back information from the press. And if that's the case, who knows what else they might know that they aren't divulging?"

Hannas-ma wanted to come back with a quick retort, but instead he sat tight-lipped, directing his displeasure inward, knowing full well that Levdroko was right.

"NINE MM PARABELLUM, probably from a Beretta," John Kissinger said, skimming through the confidential police report on the killings of the two park workers. "They were shot from behind."

"Figures," Lyons said. He sipped from a Styrofoam cup filled with an elixir of high-protein drink and liquid vitamins that supposedly helped to cut down on the adverse effects of jet lag. He'd arrived in Mammoth less than an hour before, along with Jack Grimaldi, Pol Blancanales and Hal Brognola, who had been contacted by Aaron Kurtzman with news of the quake. Along with John Kissinger they were crowded into a small office down the hall from the emergency room at Mammoth Lakes Medical Center. Gadgets had his ankles taped tightly and was feeling the effects of a mild painkiller and anti-inflammatory medication. Kissinger had been treated for a superficial gash on his right forearm, apparently received from contact with a jagged edge of the blasted sniper's roost at the time of the earthquake. The two men had tended to their own wounds using first-aid kits provided by hospital workers, who were otherwise deluged by other victims with more serious injuries sustained during the tremor and its aftermath.

"It seems pretty clear that they were gunned down because they'd stumbled onto the site where the bomb was being readied," Kissinger went on. "Some other rangers heard the shots and were supposedly told that bears were on the loose up here near the seismological equipment, but obviously it was the killers who put the call through to buy some time."

"Any clear-cut evidence it was this Yellow River Brigade?" Brognola asked.

"Of course it was them," Schwarz muttered. "I mean, we must have hit the hatchery about an hour after they split. We've got two people who saw the Winnebago passing through Mammoth, one forty-five minutes before the quake, the other a half hour later. And that second sighting had 'em on their way to the highway."

"Going which way?" Blancanales asked.

"Don't know," Schwarz said. "My guess is they came south, figuring to stop by the hatchery."

"But that place was flattened by the quake," Lyons said. "According to the seismo maps, they had to figure it was in line to get hit. Doesn't make sense that they'd go back there."

"Then why did they leave some men there?" Kissinger wondered aloud. "They sure as hell were guarding against something when we showed up."

"Evidence," Brognola surmised. "From what I understand, there's enough stuff in the rubble to nail the Brigade for just about everything from the XT-22 raid to the plutonium theft in Cumberland and that sabotage at Wisdom Plateau."

Schwarz rose from the chair he'd been sitting in and tried walking. From the grimace on his face, the effort was obviously excruciating, and he gave up after a few steps and bitterly grabbed at the crutches that had been given to him. "From now on, I'm wearing ski boots whenever we go out," he vowed, only half joking.

Brognola asked for the police report Kissinger had been skimming. He fingered one of his ever-present cigars as he scanned the document. "From the Geiger counter readings around the blast site, it looks like they at least did a good job of keeping radiation leakage to a minimum. Hardly seems possible."

"Well, normally it would be hard to do," Kissinger explained, "but they were able to drop the bomb deep enough that the levels weren't much higher than readings they get at underground test sites in Nevada."

"And how'd they get the warhead down that far?" Brognola wanted to know. "According to what it says here, that scintillation counter shaft they used was nowhere near deep enough."

"It wasn't, at least not on its own," Kissinger said.

"Meaning what?"

"Meaning that the shaft was just the starting gate," Kissinger replied. "They lined up a laser system and used that to drill the rest of the way down."

"Laser system?" Brognola echoed. "When did a laser system come into the picture? I don't remember hearing about any of those being missing."

"That's because no one knew one was stolen," Kissinger answered. "The one they used was supposedly destroyed a couple of months ago down in Pasadena, along with the guy who created it." He went on to explain the circumstances surrounding the mysterious "demise" of Dr. Shih Consai and the disturbing parallels to the disappearance of Kissinger's onetime weapons partner Howie Crosley.

12

Paranoia feasted on Oleg Levdroko's mind, as it always did when a major venture was finally put into motion and had reached the stage from which there could be no turning back. Each phase of the operation brought with it new variables, more balls to be juggled, and for the Russian it seemed that with each step taken forward the odds increased that failure would quickly follow, spawned by some slight miscalculation that would snowball into a blunder of irreversible magnitude.

Obsessed with the notion that this time his undoing was in the making because of the evidence left behind in the wake of the Mammoth Lakes quake, Levdroko called back to the San Francisco desk with orders to have his most trusted operatives dispatched forthright to Owens Valley. He hoped they could somehow pry through the official silence concerning the deaths of the two park service employees slain by Jon Yang.

Levdroko was further concerned that there had been no response from Montgomery Landlicott and the two Yellow River Brigade members left behind at the hatchery near Big Pine. They had been charged with providing reports as to the first official response to the quake and also with carefully packing the laboratory

Schwarz picked up at the end of Kissinger's remarks. "When we looked through what was left of the hatchery, we found ample proof that Shih Consai is alive and in cahoots with the Brigade. Not to mention Dr. Yurvi. And since they both got away in that Winnebago, it's a safe bet that they plan to strike again."

"Again?" Grimaldi said. "You mean they didn't shoot their whole wad causing this quake?"

"Hardly," Kissinger replied. "Near as we can figure, they probably still have enough plutonium and warheads to come up with another two or three bombs. I hate to say it, folks, but my guess is that this quake was just the warm-up act. The worst is yet to come."

materials of Robert Yurvi and Shih Consai for transfer from Big Pine to a KGB safehouse near Reno, Nevada. However, the fact that no such response had been forthcoming, coupled with news that the hatchery was located in the vicinity of the heaviest reported quake damage, led Levdroko to believe that perhaps the three men had been forced to flee due to unanticipated damage to the hatchery or some other even more ominous circumstance.

But it would be several hours before his operatives had access to any breakthrough information on that front, so Levdroko forced himself to concentrate on more immediate concerns.

Although at the hatchery it had been possible to receive directly satellite data transmitted from the Ventura Quakesim system, at Evertt mansion a more cumbersome means of receiving the same information was being employed. This was primarily out of concern that by now United States intelligence had no doubt marshaled its forces enough to pinpoint any transmission being beamed down to an American receiver from a Soviet satellite. Accordingly, the intercepted Quakesim signal was being diverted to a Soviet receiving station in Kamchatka, near the Bering Sea. From there, the information was translated into code before being relayed by radio signal to special antennae rising from the grounds of the Evertt estate. This procedure resulted in a two-hour time lag and provided Shih and Yurvi with only a fraction of the information they had had access to in Big Pine, but the security risk was appreciably lower.

A team of technicians was in the process of readying the antennae behind the guest house when Levdroko wandered out to watch them, smoking a thin brown-papered cigarette. Hannas-ma Yang was already there, sitting back in a redwood chaise longue and staring up at the cloud-patched sky.

"So hard to believe that the sky can look so clear and yet be filled with so many different kinds of signals," Hannas-ma observed as Levdroko strode into view and sat in the chair beside him. "It still amazes me that anyone was able to find a way to do all these things we take for granted today."

Levdroko stared at the sky for a few moments, finishing his cigarette. He wasn't interested in Hannas-ma's conceptual musings. "I want us to keep our momentum," he said, turning to the shorter man. "Is there any reason we can't strike another target tomorrow?"

Hannas-ma frowned. He slowly sat up and glanced at the Russian. "Tomorrow? The plan was to wait until later, to coincide with the launch. Why change?"

"Our agents at Vandenberg say they've moved up the launch date because of the weather," Levdroko explained. "A storm's predicted to be coming in by week's end, so they want to make sure they don't have to postpone again."

"They have everything ready?"

"Yes," Levdroko said. "The satellite has been ready for almost a week now."

The satellite he was referring to was the EK-2 Nomad, an orbital communications and surveillance system destined to replace the KH-12 as the United States military's primary eye in space. The new satellite's capabilities not only dwarfed those of any comparable system, but also had been specifically built to

and masked, that would help to neutralize opposition to a Soviet-China pact and of marshaled clandestine forces that would surface and be put under the command of the Yellow River Brigade when the time came to seize power from those who might still have the audacity to resist what Levdroko assured Hannas-ma would already be a fait accompli. All in all, the KGB official's plot was a pathetically frail fantasy, most certainly doomed from the onset, but Levdroko had done his homework on Hannas-ma Yang and knew how to weave the tale in such a way that the Chinese terrorist's insatiable ego and pride would be fed sufficiently to blind him to the fact that he would be squashed with brutal finality within moments of making his first move against the existing Chinese politburo.

From the fanatical gleam in Hannas-ma's eyes, Levdroko felt certain that the terrorist had once again been adequately stroked and baited so that he would carry out the final task the KGB would ask of him. The technicians had the twin antennae readied, so Levdroko suggested that he and Hannas-ma proceed to the nearby guest house, which had been transformed into a laboratory for the two scientists most responsible for the execution of the Soviet plan. Dr. Yurvi was hard at work preparing another XT-22 warhead and Shih Consai was studying topographical maps along with the last Quakesim readings taken from the hatchery communications setup.

"I want to know this material inside out," Shih explained to Levdroko and Hannas-ma, "because the new readings we get won't have nearly as much visual detail. I'll have to integrate their code signals into readings here and simulate the effect.'' He pointed to a nearby computer rigged with a sophisticated graphics program that had allowed him to reproduce the image on the sheet of paper he was holding.

"But you will be able to pinpoint our next target with as much accuracy as in Mammoth?"

"Close enough," Shih promised. "Watch, we're just starting to get our first signals, so I can give you an idea of how it works."

The radio receiver linked to the antenna was roughly the size of an upright piano and filled with so many fine-tuning and filtration switches that it took two technicians to effectively draw in the signal being sent out from the Kamchatka station now receiving data from the Quakesim HO-29. The broadcast was in Russian and was frequently interrupted by bursts of static.

"It's just weather information," Levdroko said, picking up a bit of his native Russian.

"Yes and no," Shih Consai said, sitting down at the computer console and punching a series of commands on the keyboard. "The vocal transmission is totally benign. Weather reports, as you say. It's the static that contains the code."

"The static?"

"Yes. Look."

Hannas-ma Yang and Levdroko huddled behind Shih and stared at the computer screen, which displayed a miniaturized image of California that directly corresponded with the Quakesim replica in Ventura. Each time the radio emitted a blast of static, there would be a discernible change on the screen, representing geological shifts noted by the Quakesim's network of monitoring stations. Further, Shih was able to isolate any given area of the screen and produce blowups of those locations where the most activity was taking place.

"Amazing," Levdroko said, watching the wavering flicker of graphics on the screen. "So you can call up the Traverse Range and see how the fault system there has reacted to the quake at Mammoth?"

"Exactly," Shih said, even as he was typing the necessary commands to bring the image in question into view. He pointed to an area in the foothills just north of Santa Barbara. "From the looks of it, this may turn out to be the best place to strike. Of course, this could change by tomorrow or—"

"Excuse me, sir," a lean-faced young man interrupted, striding up to Levdroko. "You have a long distance call from Ventura. Hound Dog. He said it was urgent."

Hound Dog was Mel Bronson.

Levdroko excused himself from the others and went into a bedroom adjacent to the laboratory. The telephone there was linked up with a scrambler, clearing the line from the possibility of eavesdropping.

"Hound Dog," Levdroko said. "You've done an admirable job so far. I hope you have more good news to report."

"I wish." Bronson's voice was strained. "We've got problems."

"Oh?"

"They're pulling all kinds of computer experts out of the woodwork and putting them to work on the Quakesim," Bronson reported. "Some female whiz and a guy in a wheelchair who's got more on the ball than anybody I've ever seen! Hell, even my wife's up here helping out. It's all I can do to stay one step ahead of them."

"But you *are* staying ahead of them," Levdroko said.

"For now," Bronson replied. "I can't fool 'em for much longer, though. My guess is they'll have the Quakesim back on line here sometime tomorrow morning."

"That's too soon!" Levdroko said. "You need to keep them from getting any data until at least tomorrow night."

"You aren't hearing me," Bronson complained. "If I keep tinkering, they're going to be onto me by the end of the day, then you'll really be finished."

"Then maybe you'll have to do something to keep them out of your hair," Levdroko suggested.

"Like what?"

"Whatever is necessary," Levdroko said. "Need I remind you that in addition to your computer training, we taught you a few other things about neutralizing the enemy."

13

In a free society watched over by vigilant media privy to contacts and surveillance techniques that rival those of the most advanced intelligence organizations, it's no small wonder that government secrets and skeletons supposedly hidden in the closets of public figures invariably reach the headlines and the evening news. So it was with the recent crisis Able Team had been drawn into. No matter how much of an effort was made to suppress or at least downplay the precipitous events of the previous few days, the press was too observant not to catch wind of something seriously amiss. Once leads were sniffed out, the overall story began to leak to the public. In this case, thankfully, the story had been only partially pieced together. It was bad enough that a ground swell of panic was being whipped up by the revelations that right-wing Chinese terrorists were on the loose inside America's borders with several nuclear warheads at their disposal.

"If it comes out that those bastards are using the bombs to set off earthquakes, we're going to have real hysteria on our hands," Lyons complained, setting aside the morning paper.

He was sitting with the other men from Stony Man Farm in their hotel suite at Mammoth Lakes. A half-emptied tray of breakfast rolls and fresh fruit lay on the table the men were sitting around. The six of them had already downed three pots of coffee, but fatigue was still etched in their faces.

"I wonder who's been leaking all this info, anyway," Lyons added.

"Perhaps no one," Brognola observed, spreading butter across a flaky croissant. "There's still a lot of information they haven't reported. The whole thing at the hatchery, the likelihood that Shih Consai's alive, the Brigade's link with all this Quakesim sabotage.... I think that some reporters just had their feelers out at the right place at the right time."

"But let's not kid ourselves," Grimaldi said. "We all know how these things work. You get a few thousand reporters on the scent of the same story and they're going to bowl over any stonewalling efforts. If we don't get a handle on this thing and put the Brigade out of commission soon, California's going to be one big freak-out. Can you imagine what would happen if seven million people decide they have to get out of Los Angeles because they're afraid some quacks are going to goose the fault line with mini nuke bombs?" He shook his head warily at the image as he dunked his doughnut into what was left of his coffee, then swallowed the soggy ring. He turned to the others. "I say we bust our buns and come up with a battle plan, then go for it full barrel.

"I've already been in touch with some Air Force people about flying some recon over the Rockies," he went on. "How about if me and Cowboy tap into that end?"

"Sounds fine," Brognola said. He opened a manila folder and leafed through the nine pages of notes he'd scribbled over the past few hours while making calls to various agencies involved with the crisis. "As for me, I'm going to fly down to Los Angeles and try to coordinate things with the FBI. And Able Team— I want you to fly down to Ventura. Schwarz can throw in with Bear and the other folks trying to bring the Quakesim computers back to life. Pol and Ironman can hang loose and be ready to jump at any leads we might get on where the Brigade plans to strike next."

"Why send 'em all to Ventura?" Grimaldi asked. "Wouldn't it be better to spread 'em out?"

"Maybe it's because they call us Able *Team*," Lyons cracked. "Hell, the Three Musketeers didn't run off in three directions when there was trouble. We're all for one..."

"...and one for all," Grimaldi said. "Yeah, yeah, sorry I asked." He took two more doughnuts and wrapped them in a napkin as he rose to his feet. "Come on, Cowboy, let's get cracking."

Kissinger stood up and nodded a farewell to his comrades before following Grimaldi out of the room. The two men strode down a carpeted hallway to the elevators and rode to the ground floor. Out in the lobby, they saw several reporters huddled together near the phones. One of them broke away from the others and nonchalantly approached Kissinger and Grimaldi.

"You guys are part of some secret task force dealing with this terrorist group, aren't you?" the reporter asked, waving a portable cassette recorder at the men.

"That's right," Grimaldi replied with a straight face. "I'm Batman and this is my partner, Robin. We're just on our way to the Batmobile, so if you'll excuse us..."

The reporter kept stride with the two men, shadowing them out of the hotel, not about to be put off by their sarcasm. By then several other reporters were bringing up the rear. One of them shouted, "We have several eyewitness reports of Army helicopters landing near a fish hatchery in Big Pine just after the quake, yet there's been no official statement of why they were in the area."

"That's the first I've heard of it," Kissinger said, "but my guess is they were called in to respond to the earthquake."

"But they were on the scene within seconds of the tremor," another reporter badgered. "From our information, the nearest base for the Apache and Chinooks is way down in China Lake. They couldn't have been responding to the earthquake unless they knew it was coming. Could it have something to do with that sabotage to the monitoring station at Wisdom Plateau?"

Grimaldi and Kissinger stopped at the edge of the parking lot and faced off with the press. "No comment," Kissinger insisted. "Okay?"

"Then there is a connection," a pressman surmised.

"No comment," Kissinger reiterated. Glancing over the heads of the reporters, Cowboy saw Brognola and Able Team slipping out of the hotel and heading for second parking lot adjacent to the main building. He decided to buy them some time and told the media, "You gentlemen are all barking up the wrong tree here. If you're looking for information, I believe that there's going to be a press conference held at the hospital in a couple hours. Any updates on the situation will be spelled out then, okay?"

"Then you won't confirm or deny a link between the quake and the terrorists?" a reporter persisted.

"Our objective here is to deal with existing problems, not create new ones," Grimaldi said. "Now, please..."

The pilot slid into their rental car and Kissinger got in the other side. The reporters continued to shout questions as Grimaldi backed out of his parking spot, then drove off, leaving them behind.

"It's about to blow," Kissinger muttered, staring at the other men in the rearview mirror. "The worms are out of the can."

As THE LATEST Quakesim readings came into the clandestine laboratory at the Evertt mansion, Shih Consai noticed an evolving situation that he hadn't counted on. Whether it was mere coincidence or a direct result of the Owens Valley quake, all incoming data pointed out an unexpected increase in instability along the tectonic plates in Northern California.

"Look here," Shih told Oleg Levdroko, indicating the computer screen, where he'd called up an image of one-hundred-square-mile area around San Francisco Bay. By tinkering with the graphics mode, he was able to highlight the network of north-south fault lines that ran parallel to the coast in that vicinity. Pinprick dots of light bleeped along the jagged lines on the screen.

"And it's not just San Andreas," Shih explained. "The San Gregorio, the Hayward, the Calaveras...nearly every single fault in that entire region shows signs of potential unlocking."

"Meaning what?" Levdroko asked, deliberately lowering his voice so as not to draw the attention of the others in the laboratory. The two men were alone at the computer, Hannas-ma Yang having departed moments before to consult his brother and other members of the Yellow River Brigade about their pending assignment in Santa Barbara.

"Meaning that if we go ahead and let loose with another bomb down near the Traverse Range we might wind up with more than we bargained for," Shih said.

"But I thought that since the faults weren't directly linked, that wouldn't be a problem," Levdroko said, only beginning to grasp the total repercussions.

"That had been my estimate," Shih Consai conceded. "But you have to realize that this data reflects hard facts, not an untried theory."

"Shit!" Levdroko followed the curse with a few more choice epithets in his native tongue. He walked away from Shih Consai, ignoring the inquiring looks cast his way by Dr. Yurvi and the lab technicians still manning the radio receiver.

Outside, the KGB officer absently lit another brown cigarette and walked slowly across the vibrant green lawn. Overhead, a pair of gulls screeched noisily on their way to the ocean, but Levdroko paid them no heed. Nor did he pause to observe the Yellow River Brigade, gathered in a small circle on the patio b hind the main house. The news from Shih Consai troubled him deeply, insofar as it spelled out the enormously high price that might have to be paid if he went through with the plan to trigger a quake near Vandenberg Air Force Base. He had access to figures from the Office of Emergency Preparedness and knew the projected estimates of the possible toll a high-magnitude quake could wreak on the San Francisco area. Ten thousand dead and forty thousand injured. If dams failed, the casualties could run as much as ten times higher. To have responsibility for such a calamity laid on the doorstep of the Soviet Union would without question be grounds for a declaration of war.

Was it worth that kind of risk?

As Levdroko struggled with his decision, he was called into the mansion to take another phone call, this one from his field operatives in the Mammoth–Big Pine vicinity. The news was mixed. The agents in Big Pine had managed to learn that there had been a fire-fight at the fish hatchery just prior to the quake, and that the hatchery itself had all but been destroyed by the trembler. Word was that Montgomery Landlicott and the two Brigade sentries had died, in either the fight or the quake, which meant that more than likely there had been no interrogation. However, there was enough incriminating evidence at the scene to help the authorities link Shih Consai and Robert Yurvi with the Yellow River Brigade.

"What about us?" Levdroko wanted to know. "Has anyone fit us into the equation?"

"Not that we know of," the agent reported. "We're still trying to get more information. Nikolai is posing as a reporter in Mammoth and he had a chance to question part of some special task force that's been assigned to the case. Everyone's being tight-lipped but he's positive that they know more than they're letting on."

"Stay on this," Levdroko commanded. "I must know if the KGB is implicated."

"We'll do the best we can," the agent promised. "But, as you know, the more that they look into the matter, the more different agencies will come into the picture. Already we suspect that they've got spy planes involved in searching for the Brigade, and the Air Force is trying to trace the Quakesim signal. Once they find out it's one of our satellites that is receiving the data, our cover will be blown."

"Then we will have to make sure that doesn't happen."

As Levdroko hung up the phone, his expression changed to a look of grim impassivity. It was a terrifying visage, that of a man who had forsaken conscience in the name of expediency, a man who was determined that his destiny should be fulfilled without consideration as to who might be forced to pay the consequences.

The Russian had taken his call in a study that contained many of the strategic files he had brought down to Monterey in the limousine. As he sat back at Evertt's prized teakwood desk, Levdroko opened one of the files, which concerned itself with United States intelligence efforts based on the California coast. He pulled out a map indicating the positions of the various enterprises. Six of them were of particular interest to him.

At Centerville Beach, far up the coast near Cape Mendocino, the United States Navy had its control center for Colossus, a large network of undersea, cable-connected listening devices spanning the Pacific as a means of tracking Soviet ships and submarines. Additional support in this area came from Skaggs Island to the south, where Naval Security employed its massive, so-called "elephant cage" antenna system to further pinpoint the maneuverings of the Soviet Pacific fleet. Across the bay, at Moffet Field Naval Air Station in Mountain View, P-3C Orion aircraft were ever prepared to lend aerial assistance to the nautical surveillance effort, and if warfare broke out, the fighters would be first dispatched to hunt and destroy Soviet subs. In nearby Sunnyvale was Lockheed Missiles and Space Co. Inc. and Ponsedyne Research, makers of the KH-12 and Nomad spy satellites respectively. Sunnyvale was also the site of the Air Force Satellite Control Facility, which was charged with overall supervision of the United States spy satellite program. Lastly, inland near the state capital of Sacramento, Beale Air Force Base in Marysville was the principal home of the U.S. aerial reconnaissance effort and its various stealth planes.

In Levdroko's mind, there were two common denominators to these six facilities. Combined, they constituted the lion's share of American intelligence efforts directed against the Soviet Union, and as such had been the target of an ongoing effort by Levdroko and his entire San Francisco desk of the First Chief Directorate.

Secondly, all six areas lay within range of the area most apt to feel the brunt of any major quake triggered along the Bay Area fault lines. It was by no means unlikely that a sizable tremor could disable, if not destroy some of the facilities. In any event, the damage would far surpass anything that the KGB might hope to inflict over years of isolated espionage and sabotage.

But was it worth it?

The question still loomed over Levdroko, though not as heavily as moments before. The KGB mastermind lit another cigarette and pored over the documents before him, weighing pros and cons, trying to boil down the situation into a succinct proposal he could pass along to his superiors, who would want to assume responsibility for any final decision. By the time he'd finished his cigarette, Levdroko had already made up his mind as to the plan he would propose to Moscow.

Returning to the guest house, Levdroko sought out Dr. Yurvi and took him aside.

"I should have the bomb ready in a few hours," the scientist informed Levdroko, feeling that he was answering the question for which he'd been cornered.

"Very good," Levdroko said. "And how soon could you put together another one?"

14

The smell of fresh paint was strong in the employee lounge at the California Quakesim Center in Ventura. As he waited before one of the vending machines for a cup of coffee, Mel Bronson noted that all of the plagiarized NOWAR slogans his confederates had sprayed on the walls had been covered by two coats of fast-drying white enamel. Fortunately, he thought to himself, they hadn't been able to undo the damage to the HO-29's computer with the same cosmetic ease.

At least not yet.

Ever since his call to Oleg Levdroko concerning the progress being made toward putting the Quakesim back on line, Bronson's nerves had been increasingly on edge. He knew that the KGB official was not one for idle threats, and he feared the fate that might be in store for him if he didn't find some way to detour the corrective inroads being made by the trio of Bronson's wife Rona Lynne, Lao Ti and Aaron Kurtzman. Here in the States, there was no Siberia to send people to; more often than not, the price for failure was death. Bronson knew it as surely as he knew the vending machine coffee would taste bitter and acidic no matter now much sugar and nondairy creamer he mixed with it.

He took his coffee and a shrink-wrapped tuna fish sandwich to one of the far tables, sitting down with two of his co-workers who had been victimized during the sabotage raid on the facility. The incident was still recent and newsworthy enough to dominate the conversation, and the men even enjoyed something of a celebrity status as other employees at adjacent tables queried them for details and were treated to an ongoing embellishment of the tale, in which the victims exaggerated both the size of the force that had overpowered them and the valor they had exhibited in resisting the Taser assaults that had inevitably been their undoing.

Bronson played along, though with a little less enthusiasm and intensity. The bulk of his concentration, after all, was still focused on finding a way out of his dilemma. He was already positive that he'd gone as far as he could in tampering with the computers, and there were too many people bustling about the center most of the time for him to even consider laying some sort of booby trap that might put his wife or the other two computer experts out of the picture, be it by electrocution or a less final but equally effective means. Hardened as he was by the course he'd taken, the fact that he was considering the former option with regard to Rona disturbed him. No matter what had happened between them in recent years, Bronson couldn't escape the fact that at one time he had loved the woman he had married, and there was no way he could calmly embrace the notion that he might be forced to kill her to save his own neck. Better the other two than her, he kept thinking.

It had been Bronson's hope that Lao Ti or Kurtzman could be lured away from the facility to a spot where it would be easier to see they fell victim to a "freak accident," and toward that end he had already put a call through to the men who had assisted him in the sabotage raid. He had told them to get as close to the Quakesim Center as possible and await further instruction. However, as yet neither Lao Ti nor Kurtzman had so much as taken a break from their labors in the main room, and judging from their obvious discipline and determination, Bronson had doubts they would be taking any such break in the foreseeable future.

Then, to his stunned surprise, Bronson saw Rona and Lao Ti enter the lounge, the latter sitting in a chair while she removed a pair of jogging shoes from one of the lockers beside her.

"I could really use a good eight hours of sleep," he heard Lao tell Rona, "but if I just get out and put in a few miles it should freshen me up a little."

Rona shook her head in disbelief. "When you brought along those running shoes, I thought you were kidding about doing laps instead of naps. I'm ready to drop!"

"So am I," Lao confessed, lacing the shoes. "But after the first mile I usually can shake that off...or at least I hope I can. If I can get a clear head, I think we'll make some real progress when I get back."

As Lao Ti got up and headed out of the building, Bronson rose from his chair as well and went over to the pay phone against the far wall. He dialed the number of his cohorts' cellular phone, then relayed a quick message. After hanging up, he started out of the lounge.

"Got a minute?" Rona called out, catching his attention.

Bronson slowed down, cursing himself for letting her see him. He sighed and veered over to where she was sitting. "My break's about up," he said.

"I just wanted to see how you've been doing," she said, a trace of genuine concern in her voice.

Bronson's situation being what it was, the last thing he needed was to go soft on Rona. He drew in a deep breath, then told her, "I've been doing great. Never better."

"Really?" Rona asked. "You seem so, well, wound up."

"No kidding!" he told her bitterly. "You think with all this shit going on I should be laid-back? Give me a break, Rona!"

There was a sudden quiet in the lounge and Bronson blushed as he realized everyone else was locked in on his confrontation with Rona. He avoided their gaze and quickly strode from the room, hoping that Rona wouldn't try following.

She didn't.

TWO BLOCKS AWAY from the Quakesim facility was the former Com-Tech Supplies truck. It had been re-painted, given a new set of license plates and rechristened as property of CalCoast Surveyors Inc. Parked in front of an empty lot adjacent to a busy industrial park, the truck served as cover for the three men called back into action earlier in the day by Mel Bronson.

Les Wisthepin, the gang's leader, was sitting behind the steering wheel, grinding his jaws against the wooden pulp that had once been a toothpick. He hung up the cellular phone after speaking with Bronson and reached beneath his seat for a pair of high-powered binoculars. Rolling down his window, he trained the field glasses on the side entrance of the main Quakesim building, more than three hundred yards away. He saw a petite figure emerge and pause to do a few stretches before breaking into a light jog down the shoulder of the road, heading his way.

"Good girl," he muttered, setting aside the binoculars and whistling to get the attention of his cohorts, who were out on the empty lot with a mounted theodolite and other surveying tools, maintaining their cover. "Rich, Harry, get your asses over here."

The two men came over and huddled alongside the truck as Wisthepin quickly laid out their strategy. When he'd finished talking, Wisthepin put the truck into gear and drove off while Harry and Rich wandered away from the empty lot and joined a handful of other men gathered around a mobile vending van that had pulled up in front of the adjacent industrial park. The van's aluminum siding gleamed in the afternoon sun, looking something like a spit-polished sow bug on wheels.

Rich, the taller of the two men, had the morning paper with him, and as he scanned the front page headlines, he raised his voice loud enough that the others could hear him.

"Of all the fucking nerve," he spit angrily, pretending to read from an article. He told his comrade,

"It says here those Chink terrorists might have a few agents here in Ventura. Can you imagine?"

"Shit!" Harry joined in on cue. "Maybe they're the one's that fucked up Quakesim instead of those peaceniks, whaddya think?"

As hoped, the other workers picked up on the conversation. A man waiting in line blew smoke from his cigarette and said, "Hell, it wouldn't surprise me a bit. Terrorists are ready to nuke us all to kingdom come as it is."

There was a chorus of kindred grumblings and curses from the others, and two of the men continued to fan the collective rage as they saw Lao Ti clear the slight rise in the roadway and jog toward them.

"Well, speak of the devil," the tall man said, glancing at the woman. "Could be we got ourselves a spy right here, eh?"

"I never seen her around here before," Harry added. He turned to Lao Ti and shouted, "Slow down there a minute, China doll!"

Lao Ti glanced at the men gathered around the vending van but kept jogging. However, before she could pass them, Rich and one of the other workers moved out to the shoulder of the road and blocked her way.

"We're talking to you, Mama-san," Rich said. Over the woman's shoulder, he saw that Wisthepin had re-parked the truck farther down the road, but still within close enough range to put Lao Ti in the sights of his Weatherby Mark V, a .460 Magnum hunting rifle boasting all-steel action and the ability to fire with a muzzle velocity of 1,730 fps from three hundred yards. Rich knew he had to further incite the men around him so that when Wisthepin fired, there would already be enough of a disruption in progress that no one would notice the direction the shots were coming from. The plan was for Lao Ti's death to be written off as a hysteria killing triggered by fear over news about the Yellow River Brigade's possession of nuclear bombs.

"I don't have any quarrel with you," Lao Ti calmly told Rich and the other worker. "Now, if you'll kindly move aside, I'll—"

"We ain't goin' nowhere, slant-eyes," Rich shouted, giving the woman a slight shove. "Hell, I hear there's a reward bein' offered to anyone who turns in these Chink spies slinkin' around the country."

"Oh yeah?" the man behind Lao Ti called out, reaching for the woman. "Shit, and I was just doing this to be patriotic!"

The moment she felt fingers closing around her arm, Lao Ti's patience and reticence fell away and her ingrained martial arts training took over. One second she looked as if she was off balance and about to be overwhelmed; the next, she was poised in a fighting stance and the man who had grabbed her was on the ground, wind knocked from his lungs by a fierce elbow jab to the midsection.

"I'm not even Chinese," she told the men, who had fanned out around her, hatred in their eyes.

"Yeah, right," Harry said. "If you're not some kinda spy, where'd you learn that judo shit?"

"There are a lot of women who know how to defend themselves," Lao Ti answered evenly, taking a tentative step to one side, unwittingly placing several workers between her and the distant truck. "During

World War II this country threw American-born Asians into prisons like Manzanar because of their foolish paranoia,'' she told the men. ''Haven't we learned anything since then?''

''Well, we won that war,'' Rich taunted, ''and we'll lick you yellowbellies this time, too.''

''Eight of you against one woman, I should hope so,'' Lao Ti mocked, ever on the move, weaving back and forth like a cornered animal charged with the adrenaline to make a valiant last stand.

Harry pointed off to the empty field and said, ''I say we take the little lady off for a little interrogation, eh, guys?''

''Yeah!'' Rich and several others cried out, closing in on Lao Ti. The tall man tried to jockey the mob to one side so Wisthepin could get a clear shot at the woman, but the men were moving about of their own accord and he knew he'd tip his hand if he was too obvious. As a planned alternative, however, he knew that if Lao Ti could be dragged off and worked over, she could be just as effectively put out of commission as if she were to take a slug through the heart. In fact, the way things were shaping up, it looked as if the other men were primed with enough vigilante fervor to carry out the dirty work on their own.

Lao Ti looked past the mob and called out to the vendor inside the truck, ''Call for help!''

The vendor looked at her blankly, arms crossed before him. He was clearly on the side of the other men and made no effort to intercede.

''This is wrong!'' Lao Ti told the workers as they closed in on her. ''Can't you see what you're doing?''

"Yeah, we're street cleaning!" one of them chortled. He lunged forward, reaching out for Lao Ti. She leaned away from him and torqued her body, putting her full weight into the swinging motion of her right leg, which caught the man in the ribs and sent him reeling back into her previous victim, who had just gotten back on his feet.

"You're gonna pay for that, but good!" the first man yelled.

Lao Ti found herself completely surrounded, and much as she prided herself on the recovery she'd made from her earlier injuries, she was still far from top form. Even if she had been, she knew she'd be hard-pressed to hold eight men at bay. But she had no choice but to defend herself as best she could, so she braced herself for the inevitable crush of the mob.

Then, out of the corner of her eye, she saw a Ford station wagon screech to a halt in the center of the road behind her. The vehicle's doors swung open and out jumped three men like genies summoned from a well-rubbed bottle, ready to tend to her bidding.

"Back off, fellas," Gadgets Schwarz advised, leaning on the open door of the wagon for support so he wouldn't have to use his crutches. Lyons and Blancanales were less hindered and fanned out in opposite directions, flanking the mob.

"Stay out of this," Rich advised, speaking on behalf of the mob.

"No can do," Lyons said, flexing his fingers and sizing up the enemy. A master of shotokan karate, he singled out three men he felt he could polish off and started in, figuring to make the best of his element of surprise. Sure enough, when he threw himself at the foes with a flurry of jabbing arms and legs, there were cries of pain as would-be street brawlers found themselves soundly walloped before having so much as a chance to launch a roundhouse punch. Similarly, Blancanales treated his chosen two to a near-blinding display of bojitsu and Lao Ti launched into Rich and Harry with a graceful finesse that their cruder blows were little match for.

What moments before had the makings of a one-sided rout was now an exercise in the inferiority of rampant fisticuffs when pitted against the discipline of the martial arts. When one of the would-be assaulters tried to scramble away from the brawl, Schwarz hobbled clear of the Ford and tackled the other man, dragging him to the ground.

Suddenly there was a series of loud pops and Schwarz felt the sting of asphalt shrapnel against his cheek. He'd been through enough conflict to know that a rifle had been brought into the fray, and he instinctively pushed away from the man he'd downed. Another bullet slammed into the open door of the station wagon as Gadgets threw himself inside the vehicle. Reaching across the back seat, he grabbed a holstered Colt .45 and jerked it out, flipping off the safety. Over his shoulder he could see where the last shot had hit the door, and when he retraced the suspected trajectory, he saw the surveyor's truck parked down the road and the man with the Weatherby crouched beside it, taking aim over the hood.

Wisthepin fired another shot into the mob, and Schwarz saw Rich take the bullet in the chest before crumpling at Lao Ti's feet. Harry was already down.

From this far away, Schwarz knew his Government Model was no match for the Weatherby's accuracy. He also knew that unless the rifleman stopped, his next shot might take out Lyons or Blancanales or Lao Ti.

The Ford was idling. Schwarz threw himself over the front seat and slid in behind the steering wheel, and the wagon responded immediately when he shifted it into reverse and floored the accelerator. Ignoring the raw jolts of pain shooting up from his ankles, Schwarz turned and kept his eye on the truck as the station wagon picked up speed.

Wisthepin swung his Weatherby at the moving target and squeezed off a shot that slammed through the back window of the Ford and buried itself in the dashboard a few inches to Schwarz's left.

"Nice try, pal," Schwarz mumbled as he suddenly jerked on the steering wheel and simultaneously hit the brakes. The station wagon went into a skid that brought its front end swinging around in such a way that when it came to a stop just to the left of the truck, Schwarz was a clear target for Wisthepin. By the same token, however, the rifleman was also fair game for Gadgets, who let loose with two quick shots.

The first bullet ripped Wisthepin's left hand where it was cradling the Weatherby, and he dropped the rifle even as the second shot was racing toward his throat, shattering flesh and cartilage and sending a geyser of blood surging from a severed carotid artery. Wisthepin slid against the hood of the truck, then sprawled facefirst into the dirt, next to the fallen rifle.

Certain that the man was dead, Gadgets shifted the Ford into first and inched forward to the site of the brawl, which had ended within moments after the shooting. Besides Rich and Harry, Blancanales had taken a bullet to the forearm, but he had already rolled up his sleeve and determined that it was a surface wound that looked far worse than it actually was. He had a handkerchief pressed against the gash to stop the flow of blood.

The other workers who had precipitated the near-assault on Lao Ti had either fled or were still groggy on the ground, just coming to their senses after the throttling they'd been subjected to. Behind them, the vendor was closing up his van and getting ready to flee the scene. Down the road, two highway patrol cars were screaming forward, headlights flashing.

Lyons snickered between breaths and forced a grin as he eyed Lao Ti. "Hey, lady, you sure as hell throw out one weird welcome mat."

15

Except for periodic refueling stops, Jack Grimaldi and John Kissinger had been airborne for almost nine hours straight, serving as part of a widespread aerial reconnaissance network trying to ferret out the elusive survivors of the Yellow River Brigade. With Grimaldi at the controls of a two-seater Army MH-6 "Little Bird," the two men had zigzagged over most of the central Rockies, keeping an eye open for the telltale Winnebago and responding to any promising leads from search parties on the ground. The fact that this part of the state was a vacation mecca crowded with thousands of recreation vehicles bogged down the search with innumerable false sightings. As day merged into night, the number of surveillance craft dwindled appreciably, for only those crews with access to infrared or other night-vision systems could have any hope of their flights producing results.

The MH-6 was so equipped, and Kissinger was familiar enough with the system to operate it. Grimaldi was able to concentrate on navigating the chopper, which was widely acknowledged as having the best combination of speed, maneuverability and quietness of any surveillance craft in the armed forces.

"Never would have guessed in a million years I'd be flying one of these jokers on two successive missions," Grimaldi said, fighting off a yawn. He was referring to Able Team's recent exploit near Nashville, Tennessee, where he and an old friend in the Air National Guard had commandeered an MH-6 for use in reaching an isolated hideout where an old flame of Grimaldi's had been taken hostage by renegade KGB agent Sergei Karanov.

"Well, I'm impressed with what I've seen so far," Kissinger said, keeping his eyes trained on the infrared scanner. "Maybe we'll have to twist the chief's arm and get one requisitioned for the Farm, huh?"

"That'd be sweet," Grimaldi said. "I'd like that almost as much as the gym."

By now it was after one in the morning and they were on the west side of the Rockies, passing over Jenkinson Lake and flying parallel to Highway 50, the primary thoroughfare between Lake Tahoe and Sacramento. Up ahead, the lights of Placerville winked lazily two thousand feet above sea level. They were en route to Mogtoynetti Winery, where a suspicious-looking Winnebago had been spotted near the back vineyards a few minutes before.

When Grimaldi whisked the chopper over the softly rolling hills of the winery, there was no need for the infrared scanner to see that a chase was in progress. A small, three-wheeled private security vehicle was hustling along a back road, beacon flashing, as it pursued the much faster Winnebago, which was rapidly pulling ahead and looked certain to reach the highway without being overtaken. From up in the chopper, Kissinger could see two police squad cars heading toward the scene from the east, but they were too far away to be a factor at this point.

"Going down," Grimaldi said as he pulled on the pitch stick. "Could be we're in luck."

"Let's hope so." Kissinger unsnapped his holster for easy access to his .45. At the same time he reached behind the seat for the Armbrust ATW that had served him so well back at the fish hatchery in Big Pine. If they could get close enough and it was necessary to use the Armbrust, Kissinger knew that he could put the Winnebago out of commission with one nudge of the trigger.

"I'm going to play a little chicken," Grimaldi said, fastening his sights on the back road. He set the chopper down fifty yards ahead of the approaching Winnebago, landing sideways on the asphalt. Kissinger took aim with the antitank weapon.

The recreation vehicle slowed down as it drew near to the chopper. For a moment it looked as if it might attempt to leave the road and circle around the MH-6, but when the Winnebago's headlights happened to fall upon the figure of John Kissinger grasping the lethal-looking Armbrust, the driver abandoned any thoughts of escape. He stopped the megavan and jumped out, quickly throwing his hands into the air.

As the three-wheeler brought up the rear to box the Winnebago in, six other men meekly piled out of the back of the larger vehicle, also holding their hands away from their bodies in a gesture of surrender.

Any thought that the Yellow River Brigade had been at long last apprehended vanished once Kissinger got out of the chopper and approached the captives for a closer look. Instead of Chinese, the men were Mexican, and when the backup police arrived with a Spanish-speaking officer, it was quickly established that the apprehended men were merely migrant workers who'd come to the winery at night in hopes of being first in line for work the following morning.

"That does it," Grimaldi grumbled as he pulled the copter back aloft after the matter had been settled. "I say we call it a night and start out again come morning."

"Fine by me," Kissinger said.

They were only a short haul from Marysville, so the men radioed ahead and received clearance to land at Beale Air Force Base. The small Army chopper was dwarfed on the landing field by the cream of the United States aerial reconnaissance arsenal. Three ebony SR-71s, appropriately named Blackbirds, were being readied for takeoff nearby, looking like the futuristic aircraft from a Buck Rogers film set. A more conventional-looking TR-1, descendant of the legendary U-2, had landed minutes before Grimaldi and Kissinger's arrival, and was already being prepared for another flight by maintenance crews. There were also three U-2Rs resting near hangars at the far side of the runway.

Kissinger and Grimaldi were met by Sergeant Tom Owen and Lieutenant Ned Bishop, a pair of officers from the Strategic Air Command, which was in charge of the nation's spy plane program. All four men repaired to the nearby canteen, where the two from Stony Man Farm were briefed on SAC's input into the search for the Yellow River Brigade.

Owens explained that high-altitude recon flights over California had been taking place all day and night, and that the resulting photographs were presently undergoing close scrutiny by a crew of experts who were looking not only for the Winnebago but also for any unauthorized large-scale satellite dishes or antennae that were possibly being used as part of a plan to intercept signals from the malfunctioning Quakesim HO-29. There hadn't been much luck on that front.

"And the Quakesim's still sending data out into space to God only knows where," Bishop complained. "We talked to your people down in Ventura and they almost decided to shut down the whole operation just to keep the information out of enemy hands."

"Might not be a bad idea," Kissinger mused.

"That's what they thought at first," Owen said, "but there's still some stuff that they can glean off the replica, and your guy Kurtzman thinks there's a chance he can crack the snafu in the computer by morning if all goes well."

"Well, if anyone can do it, it's the Bear," Grimaldi said.

"You guys want to crash awhile, we'll set you up in the barracks," Owen offered.

Kissinger nodded, suppressing yet another yawn. "A few winks sure could help. Just until dawn, then we're back up and at 'em."

HAL BROGNOLA HAD TURNED in shortly before midnight, and after a few hours of restless sleep, he was back up, bleary-eyed but too preoccupied with the crisis at hand to bother trying to get any more sleep. He was staying at the Airport Hyatt near L.A. International, where he'd spent most of the previous evening in strategy conferences with the FBI, the Office of Emergency Preparedness and a handful of other agencies trying to come to grips with the threat posed as long as the Yellow River Brigade remained on the loose with Dr. Yurvi and Shih Consai providing them with a means of unleashing widespread mayhem throughout the state.

As he showered, shaved and gulped down a meager room service breakfast, Brognola kept coming back to the key question that had cropped up in every discussion concerning the crisis.

Why?

What was the Yellow River Brigade's motivation? There had still been no official acknowledgment from the group that it had been responsible for the earthquake in Mammoth and the events leading up to it, and obviously still no declaration of demands. Political analysts suspected that Hannas-ma Yang had plans to use the nuclear weapons, not in California but back in his native China, as a ploy for wrenching power from the existing politburo. While this was a mildly comforting thought for those worried that the next bomb might again be targeted for the West Coast, there was no proof behind the theory, and there was so little documentation as to the specifics of the Brigade's political beliefs that no one could be positive that the terrorists weren't just interested out of sheer sport in seeing how big a calamity they could inflict upon the United States by triggering a major quake. This latter hypothesis was forwarded by a Rand think-tank member with a psychological background, who felt that Hannas-ma Yang was perhaps motivated by the same demented urges that sent mass murderers off on killing sprees.

Brognola's first order of business for the day involved a trip down the San Diego Freeway to El Segundo, where the National Reconnaissance Office had its West Coast headquarters located inside a building set aside for the Air Force Space Division. Even at this early hour, morning commuter traffic snarled the roads, and Brognola shuddered inwardly at the thought of a major quake ripping through Los Angeles while so many motorists were out. Between falling overpasses and general panic, he foresaw a carnage of crushed bodies and vehicles. Damn it, the Brigade had to be stopped!

Even more secret than the mystery-shrouded National Security Agency, the existence of the NRO was not even officially acknowledged. As such, it was no wonder they did their business in California out of a nondescript multistory building just off the freeway. Brognola had a prearranged clearance to enter the facility, but it still took him more than twenty minutes to pass through various security checkpoints before he was finally admitted to the inner sanctum of the agency, which masterminded the operational strategies for American spy satellites.

The minute he stepped into a small, smoke-filled briefing room, Brognola sensed that some major breakthrough had occurred during the night. And from the looks of it, the news didn't seem to be all that good, because the four men in the room had the appearance of hospital patients who had just received diagnostic results confirming their worst suspicions.

"Okay, what is it?" Brognola asked, grateful that in this room he could feel free to chomp on as many cigars as he desired. Two of the other men were already at work on expensive Havanas.

For reasons of security, the men's names were not offered to Brognola. The spokesman of the group, an American Indian whose rumpled suit was the same copper color as his weathered skin, told Brognola that thanks to a coordinated effort between the NSA's Yakima Research Station in Washington and the Air Force Satellite Control Facility in Sunnyvale, the errant signal being sent out by the sabotaged Quakesim Center had been traced and found to be bounding off a Soviet spy satellite for transmission to a Russian receiving station in Kamchatka.

"The Soviets?" Brognola muttered, feeling a sinking in his chest.

The Soviets.

That changed everything.

Now, instead of a band of fringe lunatics, the United States found itself staring into the jaws of its most powerful adversary. And if the Russians were somehow in cahoots with the Chinese, it was a two-headed creature with double the jaws and double the menace.

"The President has already called Moscow," Brognola was told by one of the other men, "and they deny any involvement with the Yellow River Brigade."

"Why doesn't that surprise me?" the Stony Man director said. "I take it we don't believe them."

The man in the copper suit nodded. "We've been putting everything we have into the Kamchatka link, and we just found out they're sending a radio signal to

California. The coordinates are somewhere in the Monterey Bay area. The transmission's supposedly just weather info, but we've got cryptographers looking for codes. There's an unnatural amount of static over that frequency, so they're focusing on that angle.''

Brognola assimilated the new information from his perspective as director of the Able Team effort, trying to figure out how to fit them in. The answer was obvious.

"We're just going to have to scour that bay until we find who we're looking for," he said as he reached for a phone on the desk in front of him. "Can I get a clean line out of here? I need to make a couple of calls."

16

Carl Lyons stared inquisitively at Pol Blancanales, who was wrapping up his conversation with Hal Brognola. Pol was using an Able Team communicator, the palm-size radio system created several years before by Aaron Kurtzman and Lao Ti. The device incorporated the most advanced technological elements to provide clear, two-way conversation without the security compromise that hampered other, similar gadgets. Blancanales scribbled notes as he listened to his boss, and his handwriting was so illegible that Lyons would have been hard-pressed to read it right side up, much less upside down.

"We're on our way," Blancanales said finally, signing off and shutting down the communicator.

"Found 'em?" Lyons asked.

"Close enough," Blancanales said, rising from the table in the employees' lounge at the Ventura Quakesim Center, where Able Team had been stationed since coming to Lao Ti's aid more than twelve hours before. As the two men left the small room and headed toward the main control room, Pol explained how the search for the Yellow River Brigade had been narrowed to the Monterey Bay area, adding, "Kissinger and Grimaldi are already on their way there. The chief wants us airborne and ready to detour to any blast sight that might turn up."

"All right!" Lyons exclaimed. "I was getting a little tired of sitting around here waiting for things to break."

"Ditto."

In preparation for their assignment, Able Team had already made arrangements to have at their disposal a Hughes 500-D helicopter with supplemental fuel tanks to allow for extended flight time. Lyons and Blancanales found the on-call pilot catnapping on a cot in a rear storage room and sent him out to get the chopper readied for the lift-off, then went to track down Schwarz.

The first light of day was just beginning to pour through the upper windows of the Quakesim's central room. Gadgets was working on the main computer consoles along with Aaron Kurtzman, Lao Ti, Rona Lynne and Mel Bronson. They had the key panels out and many individual computer boards had been removed for inspection on portable testing systems.

"Well, we're making some headway, too," Schwarz reported after getting the news from Blancanales and Lyons. Gesturing to the sprawl of half-dissected pieces, he went on, "The Bear finally isolated the key problem areas. Now all we have to do is hustle up a few replacement parts and reprogram the computers, then we'll be getting some in-house readings."

"Unfortunately," Rona Lynne added, "we've got to head over to a plant in Oxnard to get the parts."

"Better Oxnard than L.A., though," Lao Ti said. "We can be there and back in less than an hour as long as they get someone to open the place up."

"There's not a lot more we can do here without the parts," Kurtzman added. "Gadgets, bad ankles or not, I'm sure you want to head out with the guys."

Schwarz nodded, rising from his chair and grabbing his crutches. "Yeah. Besides, I think I've put in my two cents' worth here already."

"More than that," Mel Bronson said. "You were a big help in putting us on the right track for that breakthrough." Too big a help, he thought to himself. Ever since Able Team had arrived on the scene, Bronson had felt more and more like a cornered rat. He knew it was only by a stroke of good fortune that his associates in Ventura had been killed during the assault on Lao Ti the previous afternoon. Thus far no link had been made between him and the others, but Bronson nonetheless could feel an omen of doom in the air. Once Rona and Lao Ti came up with the parts needed to repair the sabotaged Quakesim computers, he was sure his luck would finally run out...unless he could find a way to introduce a new wrinkle to the system while the mainframe was being reassembled. It was his only hope, however faint, and he tried his best to remain calm and not betray his desperation to the others.

He turned to his estranged wife and Lao Ti. Out of necessity, he'd made great efforts the past few hours not to get into any further altercations with Rona, and while working side by side they'd managed to maintain the semblance of truce they'd called for when they were reunited the previous day.

"Maybe it'd be a good idea if you ladies made the Oxnard run together and brought along the testing equipment," he suggested. "You'll be able to check out the new boards quicker that way. While you're gone, Aaron and I can start putting this mess back in order."

"Sounds good to me," Kurtzman said. "Let's all get cracking."

Able Team headed out a rear exit and the two women went the other way to reach the parking lot. Kurtzman reached for one of the tech manuals and flipped through pages, plotting his next course of action. Bronson nonchalantly picked up one of the control boards and used a small canister of compressed air to clean the connections as he glanced around the huge chamber. A glimmer of hope came over him as he realized that for the first time since crews had gone to work repairing the sabotaged system, the room was deserted save for him and Kurtzman. Bronson knew it was only a temporary situation, for the security shifts would be switching over during the next ten minutes and the morning guards would soon be on and making their vigilant rounds.

It's got to be now or never, Bronson thought to himself.

Kurtzman had taken another control panel and was comparing it with the schematic diagram of the computer system. Bronson took advantage of the man's distraction, reaching into his repair bag for a small microchip cluster no larger than the tip of his pinkie. If he could just slip the ministrip onto the right section of the mother board, it would remain inactive during all interim check tests and not kick into action until the entire system was totally reassembled and put through its comprehensive diagnostics program. At that point, the glitch would emerge from the woodwork, so to speak, and effectively undo most of the repairs made over the previous hour. In all, however, the damage would be more severe. Up to another ten hours would be required to disassemble the computers and backtrack to the chip cluster, which was designed in such a way that it would self-destruct after it had done its dirty work, leaving behind only a residue that could easily be mistaken for overlooked specks of dirt and dust.

"That wife of yours is a smart one," Kurtzman remarked to Bronson without taking his eyes off the diagram.

"Yeah, she sure is," Bronson said as he moved in to plant the booby trap.

"You two seem to work together well enough," the Bear said. "Seems a shame you can't iron things out."

"Well, you know how it goes sometimes."

"I guess so. Hmm." Kurtzman took a closer look at the diagram, then compared it with the computer board in his hand. "That's funny. Lao Ti's got this checked off as being set up right, but the circuitry way off."

"Oh?" Bronson tried to sound uninterested, but his hand began to shake ever so slightly, because he realized Kurtzman had grabbed hold of a board he tampered with after Lao Ti had already inspected it.

"Yeah," Kurtzman said with a frown. "These sectors are going to be way off. I can't believe she could have missed them."

"Well, we've all been going at it nonstop so long, I'm surprised we haven't made more goofs."

Kurtzman shook his head. "No, I don't buy that. Lao Ti's too thorough to make a slip like this, no matter how tired she is."

Bronson took a deep breath, trying to concentrate on the task at hand, but Kurtzman's discovery had rattled him, and the minicluster slipped loose from his needle-nose pliers. He cursed under his breath as it dropped to the floor in front of the mainframe.

"What do you have there?" Kurtzman asked.

"Just a loose clip," Bronson said.

"I don't think so."

Kurtzman powered his wheelchair forward and leaned to one side for a better look at the minicluster. Panicking, Bronson suddenly lunged at Kurtzman, trying to bowl him over in his chair. He'd underestimated the man he was dealing with, however. Kurtzman swiftly raised his right hand and caught Bronson's wrist in an ironclad grasp.

Bronson tried to wriggle free, but the Bear put the full strength of his upper torso into play, twisting his foe's arm behind his back and bringing him to his knees. Even as he was doing so, the morning security shift was entering the chamber and two guards hurried over to assist Kurtzman, who glared at Bronson with a look of accusation.

"So," he seethed, "it was *you*."

MOSCOW HAD WEIGHED the proposal by Oleg Levroko and returned its verdict. Because there was a possibility that the United States might eventually link the Soviets with the Yellow River Brigade's activities, the probable political repercussions of triggering a quake so close to the population center of San Francisco were far too detrimental for that course to be pursued. However, it was decided that a controlled blast farther north along the uppermost stretch of the San Andreas fault could be expected to completely knock out the American Naval facility in Centerville Beach and perhaps even cause damage as far south as the Skaggs Island complex, without incurring the catastrophic loss of life and property that a tremor unleashed south of San Francisco Bay would be apt to inflict. Since the Centerville Beach and Skaggs Island facilities were America's key weapons against the Soviet naval force in the Pacific, both above and below the surface, it was felt that by neutralizing those stations as well as the Vandenberg launchpad in Lompoc, the Russians could gain a sufficient strategic advantage for their efforts.

The scaled-down plan was more than acceptable for Levdroko, not only because he would still take credit for having masterminded what could become the strategic coup of the Cold War era, but also because there were far fewer logistical nightmares to be dealt with. Now he didn't have to consider the matter of evacuating personnel and irreplaceable documents and equipment from his San Francisco office. And he wouldn't have to run the greater risk of premature discovery that would have come with trying to have Hannas-ma Yang's brigadiers prepare a nuclear charge within the densely populated corridor between the San Andreas and Hayward faults just south of San Jose—where Shih Consai had determined that a blast would have to originate to take out the Sunnyvale–Mou tain View military complexes. Instead, the Brigade would head up to the more rural isolation of Mendocino County.

Levdroko would have liked to see both quakes triggered simultaneously, thereby further reducing the margin for discovery that any time lag would entail, but Shih Consai had quickly and effectively pointed out that such a strategy was unworkable. Not only was there the simple fact that the Brigade had only one laser drill at its disposal—a drill that obviously couldn't be used simultaneously near Mendocino and hundreds of miles away near Santa Barbara—but with the target areas being at opposite ends of the same fault system, to agitate them at the same time would result in increased activity down the middle of the scarp, bringing on the same San Francisco quake they were trying to avoid. As it was, a triggered quake in either location would still run the small risk of dominoing adjacent fault lines.

Because of the pending launch of the Nomad spy satellite, it had been quickly decided that the first quake should be set near Vandenberg Air Force Base. Dr. Yurvi, Dr. Shih Consai and the Yellow River Brigade had left for Santa Barbara County in the Winnebago during the middle of the night. Levdroko had remained behind at the Evertt mansion, along with the technicians who would continue to monitor incoming Quakesim data and relay any significant findings to Shih.

And now, at long last, the hour of decision was almost at hand.

As he sat in the guest house laboratory, Levdroko smoked a cigarette with a seeming ease that masked his inner anxiety. The wall clock indicated that the Nomad launch was less than forty-five minutes away. Hannas-ma Yang had already put through a call to announce that they had reached their mountain destination and were drilling the shaft down which Yurvi's modified XT-22 warhead would be dropped, with its internal timer set to detonate two minutes prior to launch time at Vandenberg.

In his mind, Levdroko imagined the launchpad, with the immense, multistory, two-stage rocket standing tall and proud one moment, then toppling under the stress of the quake moments later, with a resulting explosion of more than a million pounds of propellant that would be heard for miles in all directions. It would be a catastrophe to rival the Challenger disaster, and it would set Army intelligence back as much as the shuttle failure had harmed the space program at NASA.

Yes, Levdroko mused, it would be quite a feather in his cap. His political future would skyrocket and his place in history would be ensured. Military strategists of the future would speak of particularly shrewd maneuvers as being Levdroko-like. When faced with a problem they would think to themselves, *How would Levdroko have dealt with this?*

Levdroko's thoughts had been punctuated by the bursts of encoded static regularly interrupting the weather broadcast being transmitted from the Kamchatka receiving station in his native Russia. Then suddenly, the radio signal died and the ensuing white noise jarred the KGB operative from his rumination of glory.

"What happened?" he asked the nearest technician, who was huddled close to the radio.

"I don't know," the other man replied, fiddling with various dials and switches in an attempt to bring back the missing signal. "I think it's been cut off. Something must have gone wrong."

"No!" Levdroko intoned, as if he had the power to somehow take command over unknown circumstances clearly out of his control.

As if to confirm his worst fears, outside the guest house there came the jackrabbit hammering of several M-14s, and over the sound of gunfire Levdroko could hear sirens and the unmistakable whir of helicopter rotors. Dashing to the nearest window, he glanced out and saw an MH-6 sweeping down toward guards stationed on the mansion grounds. The chopper's forward-mounted machine gun returned the guards' fire and the men on the ground dropped their rifles, contorting from the force of ammunition pummeling their unprotected flesh.

"Grab your guns and fight them off!" Levdroko shouted to those inside the guest house.

There was a scramble as the men abandoned their posts at the radios and computers and snatched M-14s and Smith & Wesson pistols before taking up positions near the windows. During the commotion, Levdroko retreated to a back room, where he reached for a lever half-hidden atop the door molding. A panel of the wall snapped loose and the Russian pried open a secret door that led to a darkened hollow in the wall, barely wide enough for a man. He wriggled along the corridor for several feet, then felt for the first rung of ladder that would take him down to an underground chamber and a tunnel that burrowed beneath the entire estate. It led to a coastal marina, where a motorboat belonging to Evertt was moored and ready to provide Levdroko with his chance to flee.

THIS TIME Kissinger and Grimaldi had their reinforcements alongside them as they closed in on the enemy. At the same time Grimaldi was bringing down the MH-6 onto the grounds of the Evertt mansion, a pair of larger OV-1 Mohawks were further disrupting the tranquility of Seventeen Mile Drive as they came in with their rotors blaring and their machine guns blazing. Ground troops from nearby Fort Ord Military Reservation poured out of unmarked vans and trucks, laying siege to the estate's perimeters. All in all, it was a morning the wealthy of the neighborhood would long remember, provided they survived the hellstorm.

While the crews from the two Mohawks focused their assault on the main house, Kissinger and Grimaldi took their cues from the newly installed antennae and made for the guest quarters. Cowboy was lugging the Armbrust again, while Grimaldi stuck with his Government Model automatic.

Within seconds of climbing down from their chopper, the men were greeted with a fusillade from the guest house that stitched small divots in the manicured lawn. Kissinger veered past one of the slain men they'd gunned down prior to landing and rolled to cover behind a redwood pagoda blanketed with fiery blossoms of orangish-red bougainvillea. Bullets followed him, splintering through the latticework that supported the bush. One round glanced off the side o his Armbrust, but fortunately at an angle that failed to detonate the loaded warhead or to disable the weapon.

Grimaldi had fanned off in the opposite direction, tumbling past the second body and outracing flak to the protection of a low stone fence surrounding Evertt's prized collection of camellias. Jack vaulted the fence on the run and used the dense bushes to break his fall as he landed hard on his side. While he paused to catch his breath, he could hear the battle being waged elsewhere on the grounds, and he was determined that he wasn't going to miss out on any more action than necessary.

Crawling on his belly, Grimaldi inched through the camellias, which provided adequate cover until a sniper on the second story of the guest house noticed the stirring of the uppermost branches and began firing blindly into the brush with his M-14. Grimaldi wriggled closer to the stone wall and rose to a half crouch, peering over his .45's phosphorous sights to draw bead on the rifleman. He had the gun switched on its semiauto mode, and it took five shots to take out the sniper, who had the advantage of firing from higher ground. When the lethal round drilled its way into his upper chest, the man slumped through the shattered window, and jagged glass bit into his torso, adding to the shower of blood that rained down onto the patio below.

Fifty yards away, Kissinger faced the same dilemma he'd had to contend with back at the fish hatchery in Big Pine—namely, that he had to choose his shots carefully with the Armbrust for fear of accidentally turning Seventeen Mile Drive and the rest of the bay into a nuclear wasteland. Instead of the building, he took aim at a gardening cart parked close to the front entrance. The cart was stacked high with large bags of fertilizer and soil, and as expected, when a direct hit decimated the small vehicle, its contents burst outward in all directions, creating both an appreciable distraction and a smoke screen of sorts, behind which Kissinger could break from the pagoda and rush the building.

Grimaldi was on the move the moment the cart exploded, and both men reached the doorway simultaneously. Cowboy had left behind the Armbrust and snatched his .45 from his shoulder holster, so that two men fired twin semiautomatic greetings to those inside the guest house. A pair of gunmen in the front hall were cut down immediately, and another four technicians inside the makeshift laboratory were wounded before they had the sense to surrender. By then more than half a dozen warriors from Fort Ord had converged on the house as well. Except for the hum of the equipment inside and the drone outside of an OV-1 with its rotors still running, the estate had fallen strangely silent.

The siege was over.

17

Far less known than its Cape Canaveral counterpart on the East Coast, Vandenberg Air Force Base nonetheless was of equal, if not greater strategic importance to the United States space effort, particularly in terms of military applications. And the latter's location near the California coastline was no matter of mere chance, but rather one of well-thought-out design. A key necessity in the placement of spy satellites was to achieve a low polar orbit, thereby allowing for maximum surveillance opportunities, and such an orbit could be reached only by a westward, relatively lower takeoff trajectory than those of eastward-launched Canaveral craft bound for higher altitudes. Given the risk factor inherent in virtually every launching, it would constitute reckless endangerment to attempt a westward blast-off from Florida that would carry a rocket and payload inland over the densely populated Southern states. One need only contemplate the compounded tragedy that would have occurred if the Challenger spacecraft had been launched over land and had exploded its shower of lethal debris down on Orlando. A launch from Vandenberg eliminated that threat, for takeoffs were directed over the Pacific Ocean and the odds of fallen objects wreaking high casualties to bystanders was rendered negligible.

And so, as they had since 1960, the ground crews at Vandenberg prepared to assist in the lift-off of yet another spy satellite, the revolutionary EK-6 Nomad. Buzzing about like ants on the sun-bleached cement slabs blanketing the base, men in hard hats attended to the countless last-minute preparations. Those workers gathered near the monolithic red launch platform at Space Launch Complex 4 were further dwarfed by the sixteen-story Titan 34D rocket that would propel the Nomad satellite onto its celestial mission. After a horrendous string of failures, most of them attributable to design flaws in both liquid and solid fuel systems, the Titans had finally been corrected to the point where the three previous launchings had gone off without a hitch. All in all, there was an air of optimism at the base.

It was twelve minutes before countdown.

"SOMETHING'S WRONG," Jon Yang said, glancing up from the radio inside the Winnebago.

"What now?" his brother snapped, nerves already frayed from earlier complications that had befallen this latest, most crucial phase of his long-range strategy.

"The signal's been cut off from the mansion," Jon said. "I heard gunfire in the background before it went out."

Hannas-ma Yang shook his head. They were so close. Things couldn't fall through now.

They were in the mountains just north of Santa Barbara, only a few miles from the country retreat of a former President and a short jog from hideaways enjoyed by several Hollywood film stars. Early rainfall had turned the hills a luxurious green, and the surrounding cover of ancient oaks and hearty manzanita provided the Yellow River Brigade with a screen behind which to pursue their clandestine chores unobserved by motorists on the nearest main road, some two and a half miles downhill.

Hannas-ma Yang glanced through the front windshield of the recreation vehicle and saw his men laboring with Dr. Shih Consai and Dr. Yurvi to ready the XT-22 for delivery down the deserted oil well they'd deepened with the chemical laser. Even that part of the operation had presented problems, with the drilling taking more than twice as long as anticipated, thereby cutting into the time they'd originally given themselves to flee from the blast site. Whereas in Mammoth they'd had the luxury of an hour to make their getaway, this time they would have only minutes—barely time enough to get down from the hills to open ground where they could ride out the anticipated earthquake the XT-22 would provoke.

"What should we do?" Jon Yang inquired, still trying in vain to raise a signal from the technicians on Seventeen Mile Drive.

"We'll carry out our part," Hannas-ma determined, forced to plot his way by instinct. There was no time for moaning and wailing over misfortune. It was time to act, to rise to the challenge of the obstacles laid out before him. He saw only one course for them to take. "Once we've thwarted the takeoff, we can go into hiding and wait to see if Levdroko is still in a position to aid us. If not, we'll have to come up with new connections. In any event, we've gone too far to turn back now.''

"I agree," Jon Yang said.

Both men got out of the Winnebago and went to join the others.

It was nine minutes before blast-off.

WORKING SIDE BY SIDE, Aaron Kurtzman and Lao Ti put their combined computer talents into the task of reassembling the Quakesim HO-29. Rona Lynne stood nearby, ashen-faced, still stunned by the revelation that her estranged husband had been consorting with the enemy all these months. She tried to focus her attention on preparing the new boards from Oxnard for insertion into the Quakesim, but it wasn't easy.

"How could I have misjudged him that much?" she wondered aloud. "To have married him without even suspecting..."

"Of course you suspected," Lao Ti told her. "You probably attributed it to something else, but deep down you must have known. You shouldn't blame yourself."

"I don't know." Rona handed one of the boards to Lao Ti. "I just don't know. To think that Mel was behind you almost being killed..."

"Hey, come on," Lao Ti said. "You had nothing to do with that."

"But still..."

"Look, Rona," Kurtzman advised her. "We've got a handle on things here. Why don't you take a breather?"

"You're sure?"

The Bear nodded. "Go on, give yourself a break."

"Thanks."

Rona got up from the table near the main console and walked slowly past the other technicians and security personnel beginning to file into the Quakesim Center in anticipation of the in-house computers' coming back on line. Looking over at the floating facsimile of California in its aqueous tank, she thought of Shih Consai and felt a further sting of shame. There was another man she'd been close to, another man who had turned out to be a traitor, going so far as to fake his own death in the pursuit of some nefarious end.

What had gone wrong with the world, she wondered. As certainly as she had witnessed the demolition of Wheaton High back in Pasadena, she now felt as if her own life were crumbling down around her. Betrayed, alone, disillusioned—she was bombarded by countless debilitating sensations, all of them compounded by her fatigue. She wanted to go off by herself somewhere and shut out the world, to close her eyes and scream until she was purged of the darkness that had come to roost on her soul.

But instead of an escape, she found herself faced with further confrontation. Heading down the side corridor, she was about to pass the main security office when the door suddenly swung open and a pair of plainclothes FBI agents emerged. Between them was Mel Bronson, his hands shackled behind his back. He met his wife's gaze and Rona was shocked by what she saw in those eyes. Or, more precisely, what she didn't see. Gone was any trace of the man she had loved and married all those years ago. Instead, she found herself staring into the eyes of a complete stranger, eyes that seethed with anger and bitterness, eyes that looked straight through her.

No words were exchanged between the two of them. There was nothing to be said.

As Bronson was led away, Rona took a step back and leaned heavily against the wall behind her. She drew in a deep breath and closed her eyes, fighting back her tears. She'd reached her breaking point and felt certain that at any second she could collapse to the floor, overwhelmed by it all.

"Rona?"

She opened her eyes and saw Gadgets Schwarz standing before her in the doorway of the security office, supporting himself on crutches.

"Gadgets..." she stammered hoarsely, "I thought you were—"

"I changed my mind. It was too crowded on the chopper," Schwarz told her. "Besides, with these ankles on the fritz I'd be more apt to get in the way than help. Rona, I'm sorry about Mel...."

"Oh, Gadgets."

Schwarz jockeyed himself forward on the crutches and freed one arm so he could hold Rona. She curled into his embrace and clutched him tightly. For several long moments they stayed like that in the hallway, propping each other up, drawing strength from their friendship.

"It's all going to work out," he assured her. "Somehow."

"I hope you're right," she said once she'd brought herself under control.

"I need to see Aaron a minute," Gadgets said. "Want to come along?"

Rona shook her head as they broke their embrace. She blinked back her tears. "I'll be all right. I just want to go outside for a few minutes. Sort things out a little."

"I understand." Schwarz kissed her lightly on the cheek. "Hang in there, kid."

Rona mustered a smile. "I always do."

As she headed for the side exit, Schwarz hobbled on his crutches into the main chamber, where there was a bustle of excitement among the technicians. And for good reason. Kurtzman and Lao Ti were positioned before the reassembled HO-29 computer, watching the in-house data banks whir through their paces.

"We're back on line," Kurtzman announced proudly.

"Good," Schwarz said, "because we got a confession out of Bronson, and we're going to need to find out where the Yellow River Brigade might be triggering a blast to knock out Vandenberg."

It was seven minutes until blast-off.

"WELL, THE 34D'S a combination of the two," Air Force Sergeant Ike Nobbers was telling the flock of reporters gathered at Vandenberg to witness the launch. He pointed through the heavily reinforced glass window providing them with their view of the launchpad. "What we do is take the Titan 3B, which is a two-stage, liquid-fueled booster, and strap on a large solid-fuel rocket system. Gives more pounce to the ounce, as we like to say."

As most of the reporters hastened to scribble down the quote, one woman in the group raised her hand and called out, "I know this is supposed to have a secret payload, but everyone knows you're putting up an EK-6 Nomad, so why not just come out and admit it?"

Nobbers, a tall, square-shouldered twenty-four-year veteran, trained his intense gray eyes on the woman with a look that suggested he wished he were Superman and had the kind of heat vision that could reduce her to a pile of ash. Below the eyes, however, he offered the most gracious of smiles and confessed, "Okay, you're right. We're putting up a Nomad."

There was a chorus of startled gasps from the other reporters, and even the half-dozen Air Force officers sharing the observation booth with Nobbers glanced at him as if he'd lost his mind.

"Yes, we're putting up a Nomad," he continued, talking in a wistful, singsong voice, "and also a KH-12, an ATACMS, a new Telstar, two turtledoves and a partridge in a pear tree." He looked over at his fellow officers and grinned. "Am I forgetting anything?"

"Yes, sir," one of his cronies shot back. "The kitchen sink from E barracks."

"Oh, right." Nobbers looked back at the woman. "We're also putting up the kitchen sink from E barracks."

"Very funny," the woman droned.

As Nobbers asked for the next question, the wall phone behind him rang. An underling answered it then held out the receiver to the sergeant. "It's for you, sir."

Nobbers took the phone and listened to the message on the other line. His look of impish mirth quickly faded and he turned away from the reporters, raising his shoulder to serve as a buffer when he spoke.

"Shit, it doesn't matter if we cancel, damn it!" he hissed. "If some quake rolls through here while that bastard's on the launchpad, it's going down ass over teakettle and we're all Post-Toasties. Forget it, we're proceeding as planned!"

"What's wrong?" another of the reporters called out as Nobbers slammed down the phone.

"Nothing," Nobbers barked. "Not a damn thing!"

"I thought I heard something about an earthquake," the woman reporter spoke out.

"This press conference is over," Nobbers said on his way out the door. "Stay put and watch. You're in for a big show!"

POL BLANCANALES and Carl Lyons tumbled out of the Hughes chopper as it pulled up into the air above the foothills north of Santa Barbara.

"Okay, let's hit it!" Lyons snapped, cradling his M-16 in his arms as he followed up the steep-pitched incline. Blancanales followed beside him as they stayed close to a horse path winding through the chaparral.

Kurtzman had called them moments before to report the coordinates of the most likely area where the Yellow River Brigade would be attempting to rig its KT-22 charge, and after sighting the long-sought Winnebago through powerful long-distance sights, Pol and Lyons had quickly devised the only strategy they felt would give them a chance of overtaking the Chinese terrorists before they could carry out their deadly mission.

The spot at which the Able Team warriors had been dropped off was three hundred yards downhill from the Winnebago and sufficiently blocked from the Brigade's view by a high-rising rock escarpment. As the two men scrambled up the slope, they knew that the Hughes chopper was being flown in clear view of the enemy and would be setting down at a point above the bomb site, in hopes of drawing the Brigade's attention long enough for Lyons and Blancanales to sneak up from behind.

It was a good plan, but Hannas-ma Yang and his underlings were not as accommodating as they might have been. With the XT-22 already dropped down the long shaft of the abandoned oil well, there was nothing left for its planters to do but pile into the Winnebago and put as many miles as possible between them and the charge before it was detonated. Therefore, when Lyons and Blancanales were halfway to their destination, they were alarmed to see the Winnebago heading down a dirt road that led away from them.

"Shit!" Lyons cursed as he broke into a run, leaving the path and thrashing through the chest-high manzanita in hopes of narrowing the gap between himself and the fleeing enemy. Blancanales forged a similar wake several yards to Lyons's right. Both men quickly realized the futility of their effort, however.

"We'll never catch up with them!" Lyons grimaced as a branch of chaparral bent and slapped him across the face, raising a welt along his jawline. Reaching a clearing, he dropped to a firing crouch and drew aim on the Winnebago with his M-16. He was about to pull the trigger when he shook his head and stood back up. "No way I'd hit 'em from this distance! Damn!"

"Hold it," Blancanales said, "we might be in luck. Look."

Lyons looked in the direction Pol was pointing and saw the Bell chopper floating back into view from behind a hillock five hundred yards away. The pilot had apparently scrapped his orders in light of the Winnebago's departure and had chosen a less passive course of action.

"That idiot'll get himself killed!" Lyons said as he watched the 500-D swoop down close to the recreational vehicle, trying to badger it off the road.

"He's buying us time," Pol said, thrashing back into the chaparral. "Let's at least show him a little gratitude!"

The two men resumed their charge through the manzanita, closing in on the Winnebago, which was being slowed down considerably by the darting presence of the chopper. The front window on the passenger's side of the vehicle rolled down and Jon Yang leaned out with his M-14, but because the Winnebago was still rolling down the steep, uneven slope, there was no way for the terrorist to fire with any accuracy and the Hughes was able to avoid taking any direct hits.

Closer to the bottom of the grade, the dirt road began to zigzag around boulder formations, giving Blancanales and Lyons still more time to close the distance. At one point Lyons dropped back to his firing crouch. Now close enough to his target to have his shots count, he directed a spray of 5.56 mm ammo at the undercarriage of the vehicle while Blancanales continued to rush forward.

Barreling along with a muzzle velocity of 1000 meters per second, Lyons's M-16 salute scarred the bottom of the Winnebago and butchered the left tires just as the vehicle was negotiating a particularly sharp right turn. The laws of physics lent a hand in the cause, and the Winnebago was thrown wildly off balance, swerving off the road and slamming into boulders the size of dozing elephants.

Blancanales was less than forty yards away when Jon Yang staggered out of the Winnebago with his M-14, followed by another of his cohorts. Using his .45 Colt Government Model, Pol beat the enemy to the draw, felling both men in the same blast of semiautomatic fire. Lyons drilled the sides of the stalled vehicle with his M-16, hemming in the others.

Overhead, the Hughes 500-D flew in tight circles like a predatory vulture. In reality, the craft was serving as an aerial marker for the two highway patrol choppers and an Iroquois from the Santa Barbara National Guard compound. The three other copters were only specks in the distance and it would be at least two minutes before they would be on the scene. Lyons and Blancanales knew that with the bomb set and the Vandenberg launch in its countdown phase there was no time to be lost waiting for reinforcements.

"You take the left," Lyons told Blancanales as he circled off to the right.

Both men cautiously approached the still Winnebago, unable to see anyone inside but knowing that the two men killed so far weren't the only passengers

When Pol was less than twenty yards away, the front windshield of the vehicle shattered as Hannas-ma Yang fired out at him. A bullet rushed past Blancanales and chipped shrapnel off the boulder behind him. Pol rolled to his left and came up firing. He put three shots into Hannas-ma as the Brigade's mastermind attempted to bolt from the driver's seat into the chaparral.

The terrorist buckled to the ground, wincing from the pain of his wounds. He looked up at the approaching figure of Blancanales, eyes burning with hatred and frustration. His dreams of glory were dying, and Hannas-ma knew now that all he had left to salvage was his distorted sense of self-dignity. Grinning through his pain, he clutched his handgun and placed the barrel against the underside of his chin, aiming up toward his brain. His maniacal laugh was drowned out by the explosion of gunfire that all but severed his head from his torso.

As Blancanales and Lyons converged upon the Winnebago and aimed through the shattered window, the remaining brigadiers threw up their arms in surrender, as did Dr. Yurvi and Shih Consai.

"Out," Lyons commanded. "Slowly. Hands on our heads."

There was a slow, solemn procession as the survivors climbed out of the Winnebago and stood next to their fallen comrades. With Hannas-ma and Jon Yang slain, they were leaderless and without the will to resist their captors.

Having seen the photos of the scientists, Lyons quickly drew the two men aside. "The bomb," he said. "Can it be stopped?"

"No," Shih Consai said with an evil laugh. "You're too late."

"He lies," Yurvi countered.

"Shut up!" Shih turned to Yurvi and spit in the Romanian's face. "Spineless cur!"

Lyons gave the Chinese scientist a brutal shove into the side of the Winnebago and motioned for Blancanales to keep an eye on him. Turning back to Yurvi, he said, "How do we stop it?"

Yurvi sighed. His face was one of resignation, even relief. "Inside the van," he muttered. "There's a remote control switch that can override the XT-22's timing system."

"Well, let's get it, pal." Lyons jerked open the door to the Winnebago and trained his M-16 on Yurvi. The scientist inched past him and leaned into the disheveled interior of the vehicle, reaching for a small black box on the floor.

"Wait!" Lyons stiff-armed Yurvi and grabbed the box himself. "How do I know you won't be detonating it instead of disarming it?"

"You don't," Yurvi said. "You'll have to trust me, that's all."

"Trust you? After all you've done?"

"Maybe I've seen the error of my ways."

"And maybe you figure on seeing how many of us you can take out with you."

Yurvi shrugged. "It's your decision."

Lyons looked deep into the other man's eyes, trying to discern his motives. During all the years he'd been the chief strategist in the field for Able Team, there had been few times when he'd been faced with such monumental choice. In his hands he knew that he held quite literally the fate of thousands.

Finally he handed the switch box to Yurvi. The scientist calmly flipped two switches and turned one dial, then handed the unit back.

"There," he said. "It's done."

There was a moment of unearthly calm, then a muffled roar sounded far off in the distance. Both Lyons and Blancanales had experienced earthquakes during their years in Southern California, and the faint rumble had an ominous familiarity. They braced themselves instinctively for the tremor and glanced uncertainly at the boulders surrounding them, which looked dangerously prone to starting landslides in the event of a quake.

Lyons muttered to Yurvi, "You bastard!"

"It's not what you think," Yurvi replied calmly. He glanced down at his watch. "It looks like they moved up the launch by a couple of minutes. Probably wanted to get it up before the quake."

Lyons warily looked westward, and slowly the tightness in his chest began to subside. Far off against the horizon, a wide, vertical contrail stretched up into the air, marking the flight path of the EK-6 Nomad, bound from the launchpad at Vandenberg Air Force Base for its eventual orbit far above the earth.

"All right!" Lyons gasped aloud in a burst of relief.

"Hey, amigo," Blancanales called out to Lyons, "I think we saved the day, yes?"

"*Sí,*" Lyons muttered, mimicking his friend's Hispanic accent and letting the tension leave him in one long, sustained breath. "*Sí.*"

EPILOGUE

Hal Brognola finished his call to the White House and joined his men in the employees' lounge at the Quakesim HO-29 center in Ventura. Able Team, Aaron Kurtzman, Jack Grimaldi, John Kissinger—the sight of them all together was enough to stir a rush of pride in the breast of their middle-aged commander. As many a time before, they'd served well and hard, pitting themselves against a merciless foe and emerging victorious... for the most part.

"Levdroko's still at large," Brognola informed the group as he stood before them to report on his conference call with the President and heads of the emergency task force dealing with all aspects of the now-neutralized threat of the Yellow River Brigade. "And Moscow still denies involvement, even when we showed them proof that their satellite was siphoning off the Quakesim signals and passing the info to the Brigade."

"Figures," Lyons muttered. "I would have been surprised if they owned up to it."

Brognola went on, "Our contacts in mainland China say there's a major cleanup going on and the Yellow River Brigade will be rubbed out by the end of the week."

"So much for a united Russian/Chinese front," Blancanales said. "Gee, it really breaks my heart that we won't have that to deal with."

"Yeah, tough break," Kissinger deadpanned.

Brognola checked his watch. "Well, gents, that plane should be about ready for us by now. What say we shove off?"

"I say let's do it," Kissinger called out. "The sooner the better."

"Solid ground, here we come," Schwarz said, hoisting himself up on his crutches. He let the others file out of the room before him, then brought up the rear as they started down the hallway. Out in the parking lot, a shuttle bus was idling near the exit, ready to take them to the airport for their flight back east. Before getting in, however, the men paused to exchange farewells with Lao Ti and Rona Lynne, who were packed and ready to head back to Pasadena by car.

"Lao Ti's going to be staying at my place for a while," Rona told Schwarz as they moved away from the others. "I think it'll be good for both of us."

"I think so, too," Gadgets said. "Lao's a great person. You two should hit it off well."

Rona looked down at Schwarz's bound ankles. "How are you feeling?"

"I'll soak 'em for a few days, then do some rehab and I'll be good as new," Gadgets promised.

"Can't keep a good man down."

Gadgets smiled. "Something like that. And listen, I want us to stay in touch, too. Let's not let another couple of decades get away from us, okay?"

"Okay."

They exchanged an embrace and a light kiss, the kiss of close friends, then Schwarz moved over to share a similar farewell with Lao Ti, who was planning to stay in the States in conjunction with her work on the earthquake studies programs at Cal Tech. There had been more invitations to rejoin Able Team back at Stony Man Farm, but she insisted that she'd found a niche she felt happy in...at least for the time being.

"Hate to rush you folks," the shuttle bus driver finally called out from behind the wheel of his vehicle, "but if you want to catch your plane, we'd best be heading out."

Kurtzman was transferred up by hydraulic lifters, then the others piled in and waved at the two women standing near Rona's station wagon.

"They're quite a bunch, aren't they?" Rona said as she returned a wave of her own.

Lao Ti smiled and said, "Yeah. They're the best."

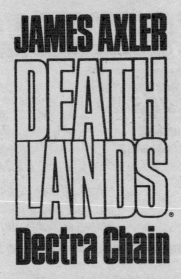

TAKE 'EM NOW

FOLDING SUNGLASSES
FROM GOLD EAGLE

Mean up your act with these tough, street-smart shades. Practical, too, because they fold 3 times into a handy, zip-up polyurethane pouch that fits neatly into your pocket. Rugged metal frame. Scratch-resistant acrylic lenses. Best of all, they can be yours for only $6.99.
MAIL YOUR ORDER TODAY.

Send your name, address, and zip code, along with a check or money order for just $6.99 + .75¢ for postage and handling (for a total of $7.74) payable to Gold Eagle Reader Service. (New York and Iowa residents please add applicable sales tax.)

Remove from pouch...

unfold once...

Gold Eagle Reader Service
901 Fuhrmann Blvd.
P.O. Box 1396
Buffalo, N.Y. 14240-1396

unfold twice...

and they're ready to wear.

GES-1A

Offer not available in Canada.